DUEL OF SHADOWS

Eli Lowenstein has been murdered, and Sam Murray wasn't the man who took his life. But when the accusers threaten to look in his saddle-bags, he remembers the strange noises he heard that night, and the talk of the planted evidence that had condemned Ephraim Harris to an untimely lynching. He's sure that if they find anything he'll swing from the end of a rope, just like old Ephraim. And there's no way Sam Murray is going to sit back and let them slip that noose over his head . . .

Books by Billy Hall
in the Linford Western Library:

KID HAILER
CLEAR CREEK JUSTICE
THE TEN SLEEP MURDERS
KING CANYON HIDEOUT
MONTANA RESCUE
CAMBDEN'S CROSSING
WHEN JUSTICE STRIKES
THE TROUBLE WITH THE LAW
SANDHILLS SHOWDOWN
KID PATTERSON
COWARD'S CARNAGE
CASTOFF COWHAND
EAGLE'S PREY
HARD AS NAILS
TEMPTATION TRAIL
DAKOTA DEATH
RUSTLER'S RANGE
IN NEED OF HANGING
SOFT SOAP FOR A HARD CASE
RANGE OF TERROR

BILLY HALL

◆

DUEL OF SHADOWS

Complete and Unabridged

LINFORD
Leicester

First published in Great Britain in 2012 by
Robert Hale Limited
London

First Linford Edition
published 2014
by arrangement with
Robert Hale Limited
London

A catalogue record for this book is available
from the British Library.

ISBN 978–1–4448–2067–6

Published by
F. A. Thorpe (Publishing)
Anstey, Leicestershire

Set by Words & Graphics Ltd.
Anstey, Leicestershire
Printed and bound in Great Britain by
T. J. International Ltd., Padstow, Cornwall

This book is printed on acid-free paper

1

The six horses stopped without directions from the driver. They had just climbed the long pull to the top of Tugman Hill. They knew from long experience they were allowed to stop and blow a while. They needed the rest. It was a long, hard pull, and today's stage was well loaded.

Because there were a couple ladies aboard, the men on the coach took advantage of the stop to step away into the cover of the brush that flanked the stage road to relieve themselves. As always, it was simply assumed the ladies wouldn't have any such indelicate needs to which they needed to attend. If either of them did, there was plenty of brush on the other side of the road. Ladies did not, however, normally succumb to that lack of proper decorum. That apparently was true with the two female passengers of the stage, since neither of them gave any indication of such a need.

They did, however, step out of the big Concord to stretch their legs and work the kinks out of their tired limbs. All except the driver did so. As the shotgun guard climbed down, the driver simply wrapped the reins around the brake handle and busied himself rolling a cigarette.

A collective gasp escaped all four throats as the two men who had stepped into the bushes emerged, each with his hands held high. From behind them a man with a bandanna over his nose and mouth shouted, 'Don't nobody do nothin' stupid! This here's a holdup, an' I'll shoot the first person that tries anything.'

The shotgun guard's eyes darted up to the seat he normally occupied, focusing on the double-barreled Greener he had left there. Even as he did, he knew he couldn't have risked a shot at the robber. The highwayman had too cleverly kept himself where he was sheltered by the two passengers.

'Climb down off'n there,' the masked man ordered the driver.

Shorty Whitcomb hastened to comply, aware that he was helpless to do anything else.

'Now all of ya get your hands up, and get lined up there, so's I can keep an eye on all of ya,' the outlaw ordered.

Resigned to the reality that they were about to be relieved of any valuables they carried, they all complied.

Keeping his pistol trained on them, the bandit ordered, 'Now, one at a time, you boys shuck them guns. Toss 'em out here far enough I don't have to worry about you tryin' to grab 'em.'

All four men complied in turn.

The outlaw nodded with satisfaction. He spoke to one of the women. 'One of you got a lap blanket in there?'

They both nodded.

He waved his gun barrel at the younger woman. 'You. Go get it, and don't try nothin' funny.'

Glancing at the others, the woman turned and opened the door of the stage. She reached inside and pulled out a plaid wool blanket. She stood holding it, waiting to be told what to do with it.

'Spread it out on the ground right there,' the man ordered, indicating a spot well in front of the line of passengers.

She did so, and quickly retreated to the line where the others stood. All had, by now, lowered their hands, and the outlaw seemed to be unconcerned.

'Now all of you shuck out your valuables and toss 'em onto the middle o' that there blanket,' he ordered.

As they all reluctantly complied, the outlaw watched tensely, as if expecting somebody to come up with a hideout gun. Nobody did. They threw their money and their watches onto the blanket.

The holdup man indicated the younger woman with a wave of his gun barrel. 'You. Step over here.'

'Why? What are you going to do?'

'Just do what I tell you. Now!'

Hesitantly she moved a couple steps in front of the others, stopping at the edge of the blanket closest to the bandit. She glared at him as if defying him to touch her in any way. He reached out and grabbed a necklace that still hung around her neck. 'I said all your valuables,' he rasped, pulling on the necklace.

'No! Let go of that! You can't have that! It was my mother's.'

As she protested, she grabbed the necklace with both hands, pulling against him.

'Let go of it!' he ordered.

'No!' She clung even more tightly to the necklace. Her chin lifted defiantly. There was a distinct Irish lilt in her voice. 'You worthless ne'er-do-well! The only way you'll ever be gettin' this necklace away from me is to take it off my dead body!'

'Have it your way,' the bandit replied.

The roar of his forty-five hit all of the stage's occupants with a shock as great as if they had been shot. The young lady's jaw dropped. Her eyes widened. She took a step backward. As she collapsed, the bandit ripped the necklace from her.

Shock, then anger radiated from five faces, but nobody moved. 'Anybody else holdin' out on me?' the outlaw demanded.

Five heads simultaneously denied any such holdout. 'Then throw that mouthy little biddy up on top an' get that thing movin' on up the road,' he ordered.

There was a long moment of hesitation. One of the men dropped on his knees and checked the woman for any sign of life. He looked up at the others and shook his head. 'She's dead.'

Growing impatience gave the outlaw's voice an ominous edge. 'The rest of ya'll be just as dead if you don't get movin'. Now throw 'er up on top and get goin'.'

With as much show of reluctance as

they dared display, the two passengers picked up the dead woman. The driver and shotgun guard climbed up on top. Reaching over the side they took the woman from the two who hoisted her as far as they could, and hauled her body onto the top of the stage.

The driver settled into his seat as the two men and one woman climbed back inside the coach. Seizing what appeared to be his opportunity, the guard grabbed his shotgun and whirled toward the outlaw. He wasn't nearly quick enough. Two swift shots from the outlaw's forty-five killed him instantly. He collapsed beside the driver, head downward, his head and one arm hanging off the front edge of the seat.

'Get movin'!' the outlaw ordered the driver. 'Now!'

Unwrapping the lines and kicking the brake off, the driver yelled at the now nervous team of horses. 'Heeyaaah. Git up there!'

The stage hurtled up the road, small clouds of dust boiling up from behind the wheels. The outlaw stood where he was until they were out of sight. He holstered his pistol. Then he tied up the blanket into a bundle with the fruits of his holdup secured inside. He stepped back into the trees and brush, disappearing. The whole deadly incident had taken less than fifteen minutes.

2

The air of Big Springs suddenly crackled with tension. Ephraim Harris smiled at the big man, but there was no mirth in the smile. The faint hint of a drawl gave his words more import, rather than less. 'I reckon there's plenty room at that hitch rail yonder.'

The big man glanced at the designated hitch rail for the barest instant, his eyes darting back to challenge the smaller man. 'Yeah, but I want this here spot. I had my eye on it afore you slipped in ahead o' me.'

The challenge was ridiculous on its surface. The other hitch rail was no more than four paces away. True, it wasn't directly in front of the Lucky Drover Saloon, as the sign announced the establishment. It was also true that cowboys didn't like to walk any farther than absolutely necessary. Any cowboy worth his salt would mount his horse to ride across the street, rather than walk. Still, it was sheer inanity to make an issue of it.

The big man had still been on the far side of the nearly empty hitch rail before Eff, as his friends knew him, had dismounted and flipped the reins of his horse at the last space on the nearer one. That gave him every right to tie his horse there.

That clearly wasn't the issue. The big man was spoiling for a fight for any reason, or no reason. He just as clearly expected the smaller man to back down.

Ephraim Harris wasn't in the habit of backing down from anybody. The well-worn Colt on his hip bore witness to long and steady use. The large knife sheathed on the other side of his belt seemed, equally, a natural part of him. The steadiness of his eyes that returned the bigger man's gaze bore no hint of compromise or surrender.

Abruptly the big man's hand darted

to his pistol. It wasn't clear of its leather when Eff's pistol was directly in front of his nose. 'Better leave it right there,' he drawled, with neither haste nor tension in his voice.

The other man's face waxed pasty. His eyes widened. He knew he was fast with a gun. Really fast. He had proven as much half a dozen times, and had left slower men lying in the dirt. That he was that badly over-matched clearly rattled him.

Then his surprise gave way to anger. The ashy pallor of his face turned pink, then crimson. His eyes flashed fire, as if trying to bore holes through the calm expression of this surprising stranger. Finally, he dropped his pistol back into its holster, turned on his heel and mounted his horse. With another withering glare at Ephraim, he wheeled the horse and galloped away down the street.

Ephraim pursed his lips thoughtfully as he put his gun away. He shook his head. 'He's been in an awful big hurry to get here, just to have a drink. His horse is lathered up somethin' awful. I wonder why he was so all het up for a set-to,' he muttered. 'He oughta be rubbin' that horse down good, insteada tryin' to pick a fight over a spot at a hitch rail.'

As he stepped up onto the board-walk, he glanced at a youngish man seated on the boards, leaning back against the front wall of the saloon. His hat was down over his eyes. He appeared to be either dead drunk or sound asleep. It was pretty early in the day for a cowboy to be that drunk, but he didn't think a lot about it. He shrugged and walked into the saloon.

The Lucky Drover was the drab duplicate of countless Wyoming saloons. The heavy door that would shut out the winter winds stood clear back against the wall now, leaving only the screen door to lessen the number of flies inside. A long bar with the ubiquitous brass foot rail ran the length of one end. Several shelves behind it were liberally stocked with liquor. Above the shelves the poorly painted picture of a nude, slightly overweight woman smiled woodenly in an invitation that would only be enticing to men long-starved of feminine company.

A substantial wood stove took up considerable space in the center of the large room. A crooked stovepipe extended out of sight upward into the smoky haze toward the ceiling.

The rest of the room held scattered tables and chairs. One corner held a large pool table, where three cowboys demonstrated their limited prowess with the cues.

Ephraim glanced around, then strode to the bar and ordered a whiskey. As the bartender filled the shot glass he dropped a coin on the bar, then turned to survey the room more carefully.

'You're Circle T,' the bartender said, more as a statement than a question.

Ephraim nodded. 'Yup.'

'Thought I recognized you. In town to make up for too many lonesome months?'

'Nope. Just ridin' through. I've been checkin' on the grass on the upper slopes. The boss is gettin' antsy to start movin' stuff up to summer range.'

'I hear the grass is pretty good up high this year.'

'It is for a fact. Best I've seen for three or four years. Them beeves oughta come back down rollin' fat come fall.'

The bartender nodded. 'The Circle T's stuff usually is.'

Eff nodded. 'It's a good outfit to work for.'

'That's what I always hear. As long as you're willin' to pull your weight.'

'Yeah, well, that's only right.'

'The Double A's needin' hands pretty bad, I hear. O' course they're always needin' hands.'

'They do tend to work a fella to death.'

'You stayin' over in town tonight?'

Ephraim pulled a cheap watch from his pocket and checked the time. 'Nah, I guess not. I got a good three hours afore dark. I 'spect I'll ride part way out to the place tonight.'

'Old Mort'll get on your case if you stay in town overnight, will he?'

'Naw, he wouldn't say nothin'. But if I stay here, I ain't likely to stay sober. If I don't stay sober, I'll likely sleep late. We got a lot to get done tomorrow. If I don't stay in town, I can camp along Broken Spoke Crick. Then I can join the bunch in time for breakfast tomorrow. Seemed like a shame to ride right through town without tossin' down one stiff drink, though.'

The bartender nodded and turned back down the bar to tend other customers. Ephraim tossed off the shot of whiskey and stood still, feeling the glow spread through him. Then he strode to the door and went out without another word.

As he stepped outside he glanced both ways up and down Big Springs' main street. There was no sign of the truculent trouble-maker he had encountered on his way in. The drunk had apparently come to and staggered off somewhere else to sleep it off as well. Ephraim mounted his horse and rode out of town, riding at a swift, ground-eating trot.

He was well out of sight and sound of the town when the stage barreled down the street and pulled to a stop in a cloud of dust in front of the marshal's office. 'Hank, get out here!' Shorty yelled at the top of his voice. 'We been robbed and Ray an' little Jenny O'Neal been killed!'

The town marshal rushed out the door, even as people began running from all parts of town to hear the story. Ephraim heard none of it.

The sun was sliding out of sight behind the mountains as he pitched his camp for the night. He picketed out his horse, cooked some supper over a small fire, then rolled into his blankets. He was asleep in minutes.

As with all those who lived in the open, Ephraim Harris was a light sleeper. He would have sworn he would wake at the sound of a cricket walking across a wet leaf. Even so, the shadow that crept into his camp later that night was so still, so silent, so fleeting that he didn't stir. His horse tossed his head once, but failed to nicker or stamp a foot. The shadow paused the briefest moment at Ephraim's saddle-bags that still hung across his saddle. He had suspended his saddle from a tree limb to keep it out of reach of small animals. They liked the salt from the rider's sweat that worked its way into the leather. At any opportunity, they would gnaw at the leather in the night, seeking that salt. As silently as it had come, the fleeting shadow was gone. Ephraim slept on, unaware.

3

It was late for the lamps to still be lit in the Lucky Drover. It was even more unusual for such a large clientele to still be in the saloon at that hour.

Johnny O'Neal sat at a table in the middle of the back wall, his head slumped onto his chest. Tears streaked his cheeks and dampened his red beard. There was little conversation.

For what had to be the dozenth time, Johnny said, 'I just can't believe it! My little Jenny, dead.'

'Coldest thing I ever seen,' Shorty Whitcomb commiserated solemnly. 'Fine young girl like that. He just never even hesitated. Not even for a second. She said, 'The only way you can have this necklace is to take it off my dead body.' And he says, just as cold as if'n he was talkin' about the weather, 'Have it your way,' and shot her dead. Jerked the necklace off her head afore she hit the ground. Then he just glared at us over that bandanna on his face, like he was just hopin' somebody else'd do or say somethin'.'

'Oh, Jenny, Jenny, Jenny!' Johnny said for the countless time. 'First her ma, now her. All inside o' six months. What'm I gonna do, boys? I got nothin' left to live for. Oh, what am I gonna do?'

Silence descended on the whole of the saloon, as the two dozen or so men sought futilely for any words that might offer comfort to the grief-stricken Irishman. Over and over he kept wailing, 'First my Emma, and now my sweet little Jenny. They're all I had. They're all I had.'

'It don't seem to me he could've got too far,' a gruff voice said, finally.

Johnny looked up, swiping at his eyes with an already wet shirt sleeve.

'Well, think about it,' Gar Newberry rumbled. 'He ain't gonna cut an' run. Not him. Like Shorty said, he's just as cold as a hunk of ice in January. Cold as he is, he's gonna stop an' gloat over what he's done. He'll take time to look through all the stuff everyone tossed onto that blanket. Then he's gonna sort it out, keep what he wants or what he can sell quick with no questions asked. He'll pocket the money, o' course, then he'll toss the rest of it where it ain't apt to get found. That's gonna take some time. By the time he done all that, it had to be pertnear dark. That means he must've had a spot already set up to camp somewhere's close by. Either that, or he had to find a spot right quick, afore it got too dark.'

'Prob'ly kept some stuff in his saddle-bag,' a faceless voice suggested.

'Makes sense,' somebody in the crowd agreed, 'but that don't help none.'

'Sure it does,' Gar disagreed. 'How many spots are there close to the top o' Tugman Hill where a guy can camp and have water? If he already had a campsite set up, he wouldn't be dry-campin'. He'd sure have it close to a crick or a spring or somethin'.'

There was a long silence as every man in the room made a mental tour of the area. Being men of the West, they could all lay out an accurate map of any country they had ridden through, even if it had been years since they had been there. Finally Swede Nelson spoke. 'There's only a couple spots inside of an hour's ride from where the stage was held up that'd fit that description.'

The rest of the crowd turned their eyes on him, already knowing what he was about to say. He obliged. 'There's that seep spring in Slippery Canyon, but it's clear down in the bottom. That's pretty rough and rocky. Not much of a place to stake out a horse, or even get blankets laid out between rocks.'

Several of the crowd nodded in agreement. Swede continued. 'The only other place close is Broken Spoke Crick. There's three or four places along it where there ain't too much brush and trees and such. Any o' them spots is good camp sites.'

Again, several heads nodded agreement.

Gar spoke up again. 'The moon's just now comin' up. That's light enough we could ride out there well before daylight. Maybe just about dawn, but if we hit on his campin' spot, we'd still be there afore he's awake. Odds are we could surprise 'im right in his blankets.'

Silence pervaded as each man mapped out the distance involved and the terrain they would have to cover. 'We could do it easy,' a voice in the crowd said.

The bartender spoke up. 'There's a cowpoke that left in the middle of the afternoon. He mentioned he might camp on Broken Spoke Crick tonight. You'd have to be right careful you don't get the wrong man.'

'Sure, an' that won't be hard to know for certain,' Johnny O'Neal spoke up. 'The filthy skunk what shot my Jenny in cold blood'll sure have the necklace he killed her for. He'll not've been throwin' that away. Whether you boys ride with me or not, I'm for ridin' out there to see if I can find meself a killer.'

Half a dozen voices spoke their agreement. All but unnoticed, a soft voice in the middle of the clamor said, 'In his saddle-bag, I bet.'

Johnny stood up, swiping the wet sleeve of his shirt across his eyes once again. 'You boys what's ridin' with me get saddled up an' meet out front here in fifteen minutes. An' come loaded for bear.'

'You oughta take the marshal along, at least,' the bartender urged.

His voice was lost in the rush to the door as each man headed for his horse. Slightly more than fifteen minutes later, eight men rode off at a lope in the soft silver light of the moon.

Neither the moon nor the distance rode did anything to soften the mood of any of the men. If anything, their anger hardened and focused as they rode, though there was scarcely a word shared among them.

After the first half hour they slowed their horses to a ground-eating trot, lest they play the animals out needlessly. They had plenty of time before daylight.

It was still over an hour short of dawn when they stepped from the saddle and crept, guns drawn, toward the first of the likely campsites their saloon conversations had identified. As if someone had released the stem of a balloon, the air went out of them as they realized the spot was empty.

As they all stepped back into their saddles, one voice said, 'There's two more good spots down the crick. Ride quiet. He's most likely at one or the other of 'em.'

They sneaked up on the second target site to the same disappointment. It was clear nobody had camped there for several days at least.

Wordlessly they remounted and proceeded to the last spot on their agenda. They dismounted well out of sight of it and started to proceed when they heard a horse stamp at a heel fly. They froze in place. 'He's here, all right,' somebody whispered.

As silently as possible, they crept forward. The eastern sky was just beginning to show the first hints of dawn. That added just enough to the moonlight to give them fair vision. As they eased their way forward, the one in the lead suddenly held up a hand. Everybody froze in place as if made of granite.

The lead man turned around and whispered as softly as possible. 'He's here. I see his blankets. You boys make a circle so we can come in on 'im from all sides.'

Moving like shadows in the pale moonlight, eight men fanned out and approached the sleeping man.

It is said there are two times a man sleeps the most soundly. One is the first half hour after he falls asleep; the other is the last half hour before the dawn. It was just as the sun was readying to hoist itself above the hills that eight men closed in and shattered that deepest of sleep.

'Outa that bed with your hands up!' Johnny O'Neal bellowed, all the hurt and anger of the last few hours giving his voice an edge an avenging angel would have envied.

Ephraim Harris leaped upward, his heart suddenly pounding, a yell of surprise cut off in mid-syllable as he looked wildly around him. Angry men encircled him. Five pistols and three rifles were trained on him at near point-blank range. He raised his hands as if they had been jerked upward by some unseen strings.

'Who are you?' Johnny O'Neal demanded.

'I . . . I . . . I'm Ephraim Harris. Eff, from the C.T. I ride for the C. T. Who are all of you? Whatd'ya want?'

'We're lookin' for the low-down, woman-killin' son of a slitherin' snake what robbed the stage and killed me own little girl,' Johnny snarled.

Ephraim acted as if he would lower his hands. 'Oh! Well! You about scared the liver outa me! Somebody robbed the stage?'

'Get those hands back up! Where was you yesterday?'

'I was ridin' over toward Round Top Mountain, checkin' out the spring grass for Mort. I rode back through town, stopped, and got me a drink, then rode on up here and camped about dark.'

'Stop your jaw a-wobblin'!' Johnny ordered. 'We'll know soon enough where you been an' what you been doin'. One of you check his saddle-bags. They're on his saddle hangin' right over there on that tree.'

The sun chose that moment to peek cautiously over the rim, adding its curious gaze to the search. It provided all the light that was necessary. Garston Newberry flipped open the flap on one of the bags and reached inside. He pulled his hand out and held it up triumphantly. 'Well lookee here, would ya! Lookee what's right on top!'

A wail of anguish howled up from the depths of Johnny O'Neal's soul. 'That's it! That's my sweet Emma's necklace. Sure an' my little Jenny never had it off her neck since her momma died. I'd know that necklace if I saw it on the neck of a banshee in the darkest corner o' hell!'

He grabbed the necklace and clutched it to himself, dropping onto his knees, sobbing. His gun lay forgotten where he had let it fall in the dirt beside him.

The circle of men looked around at each other, uncertain what to do next. 'Tie his hands,' Gar ordered. 'Get him on a horse.'

Ephraim protested, 'Look, I got no idea how that got in my saddle-bag. I ain't never seen it before in my life. Honest, fellas!'

As if his words had no ability to penetrate the shell of their anger, the men appeared not to hear. His hands were swiftly tied behind him and he was hoisted onto Garston Newberry's mount. The horse was led over to a tree where a lariat was already thrown over a limb. As he was led beneath it, a rider eased up beside him and slipped the noose over his head, snugging it around his neck.

Shorty Whitcomb's voice sounded an octave higher than its normal range. 'I think maybe we'd oughta think about this a minute, boys. It seems to me the guy what held up the stage was a pretty big man. This here fella don't seem all that big to me. Are you boys plumb sure this is the right guy?'

For one small moment it seemed that reason and truth might overcome the rage that propelled events so tragically forward. Silence descended on the campsite. Unease crept stealthily into the back of the minds of most of the men.

There is, in truth and reason, a supernatural power that whispers, softly but incessantly, into the human mind. We might often wish it would shout instead. We might long for it to force itself upon those who violate or ignore it. It will not. Some great divine purpose will never allow it to override the free will of those in whose minds it so incessantly whispers.

Maybe, just maybe, one more soft voice of that reason, in just that moment, might have saved an innocent man's life. Our innate sense of justice and right screams that it should have. That small shred of reason was, instead, shattered and scattered to the morning breeze.

'There ain't no doubt in the world!' Gar's deep voice dominated the group. 'How else would Jenny's necklace get into his saddle-bag? He's gotta be the one, and he's gotta hang for it. That's all there is to it.'

Ephraim looked full into the big man's face for the first time. In the growing light he recognized his antagonist from the day before. He struggled frantically for something, anything, that he could say that would change what he suddenly understood he could not change. Despair swept over him, leaving him sagging in the saddle.

Johnny O'Neal rose from the dirt, still clutching the necklace as if it held all the memories of his two lost loves. Tears streaked his face, but his voice was steady and hard as flint. 'I get to do it, boys! For my Jenny.'

He glared at the terrified cowboy astride Newberry's horse. He strode forward and slapped the animal fiercely across the rump, yelling, 'Heeeyaaa!' at the top of his voice as he did so.

The startled animal lunged forward. Ephraim instinctively gripped the saddle with his knees, causing the noose to jerk even more tightly around his throat than it would have otherwise. As the horse ran out from under him, he kicked and jerked, trying frantically to get loose from the throngs that showed no more mercy than the eight sets of eyes that watched.

Slowly his kicking and thrashing stopped. One spasmodic twitch shook his body when it had almost stilled, then he was all but motionless, head lopped to one side, swaying only slightly.

That insistent small, silent voice of reason and right sighed across the group of men once more with the morning breeze. For that one brief moment all but one of them felt a sudden sense of shame or guilt or regret — something that made them momentarily uncomfortable.

Once again, the moment passed. 'Somebody get his horse. Stick his saddle and stuff on it and turn it loose. It'll go home.'

'Should we cut him down and put him on it?'

'Leave him to hang there,' Gar Newberry gritted. 'Let 'im be a lesson to others that there's some things you don't get away with in this country.'

Eight men rode out together fifteen minutes later, each suddenly eager to get back to the Lucky Drover for something to drown their thoughts.

4

He sat his horse easily, surveying the small town that lay before him. From the small rise at the edge of town, he could see every building in Big Springs. It looked like countless other cow towns he had known. Maybe this one would hold the chance he ached for.

Sylvester Anthony Murray had come to Wyoming Territory with a dream and a fierce determination to make the dream real. He wanted a spread of his own, a family, and a home. That's all, really. Nothing fancy. Just a solid, honest life.

Twice before, he'd thought he'd found it. Once, the savings he had so carefully hoarded to allow him the beginning he sought, had been stolen. He had chased and caught the thief. He had faced him down and demanded the return of what was his. The man tried instead to out-draw him. He wasn't nearly fast enough.

Sam, as he reduced his too-long name to, had searched the dead man's things; there was no trace of his money. It had been hidden somewhere, and it was certain the dead man would never reveal where it lay buried.

One other time he'd thought his dream was nearing reality. Then the woman he had grown to love — the woman he had thought was the perfect one to share the dream and help make it real — had suddenly died. Appendicitis, they said. That happens sometimes, they said. Nothing anybody could do, they said.

After that, everything he saw in that country reminded him of her. Finally he decided the pain would be less if he wasn't seeing all the places they'd ridden together, the scenes they had enjoyed together, the spot they had decided together to begin their ranch.

Studying the one main street and three short side streets of Big Springs,

Sam exhaled a deep and melancholy sigh. Maybe one of the outfits around here was hiring. Most outfits were this time of year. Maybe there'd be a place here where his small stake could grow. Maybe there'd be someone here to share it with. Maybe. Always it was just a maybe.

He lifted the reins. In response, the big dappled bay that knew his master so well, moved forward without being told. The packhorse that trailed behind on a lead rope simply kept pace. Again, as if reading his rider's mind, the bay walked directly to the livery barn and stopped.

The hostler stepped out of the shadows of the stable, followed by the scent of fresh hay on the slight breeze. 'Howdy, mister,' he offered in words carefully spoken, just a little slower than normal.

'Afternoon,' Sam responded. 'You got room for Freckles and Company?'

The hostler chuckled. 'Now that is a new one,' he said in that same measured cadence. 'I have heard just about every name a man could give a horse, I suspect, but I haven't ever heard one called 'Freckles'. Is the other one named 'Company', or does that just mean the rest of the group?'

'Yeah, that's his name. You don't wanta go laughin' at 'em, though. Especially Freckles. He gets 'is feelin's hurt plumb easy.'

The dappled bay nuzzled the hostler, and lowered his head as if inviting him to scratch his ears. 'Well, we would not want to give Freckles a reason to pout, would we?' the hostler grinned.

'They could both use a good rubdown and a bait o' oats.'

'I will take care of doing that. Will you be staying in town long?'

'Not sure. Any outfits hirin' around here?'

'I am sure that somebody is. Most ranches are hiring at this time of year. There might be two or three of the ranchers at the Lucky Drover. They pretend that they hang around there looking for hands to hire, but mostly I think they just like to drink beer and talk to each other.'

'I'll check it out.' Then to himself he said, 'He don't seem too swift, but he does seem to have a way with horses. Freckles just plumb took to him.'

He shouldered his bedroll, took the rifle out of the saddle scabbard, and walked a ways down the street to the building boasting a sign that simply said, 'Hotel'.

'Not too pretentious, huh?' he muttered to himself.

He checked into a room, left his bedroll and rifle inside, then started down the street toward the Lucky Drover. He was less than halfway there when he stopped in his tracks. From a little way up a side street, a voice that sounded like a young child screamed. The scream was followed at once with sobbing pleas of what sounded like a young boy. 'That's enough, Pa! I'm sorry! I won't do it no more.'

He screamed again. This time the

scream came at the same time Sam heard the unmistakable thwack of a leather strap slapping home with powerful force.

The sounds continued as he turned and hastened toward the source of the noise. He walked between two houses. He spotted a large man bending over a writhing, crying, screaming boy of about ten or eleven. 'I'll tell you when it's enough, you smart-mouthed, worthless cur of a pup.'

He raised the belt above his head to deliver another blow to the back of the helpless boy cowering on the ground, drawn up into a fetal position, wailing in helpless anguish.

As the leather strap swung back, Sam reached out and grabbed it. He jerked it from the unsuspecting man's hand, tossed it behind himself, and dropped his hand to his gun butt, all in one swift motion.

For all of his size — easily three inches over six feet — the man whirled like a cat. Without a word he sent a

lightning right hand toward the unexpected intruder's head.

Swift as it was, Sam was swifter. He
evaded it and stepped in behind it,
delivering a straight right of his own to
the bigger man's chin. He sprawled
backward onto the ground.

Instead of leaping to his feet, the man
turned quickly over and remained on
one knee. 'Who're you and whatd'ya
think you're doin' buttin' into my
business?'

'Who I am doesn't matter,' Sam
answered, trying to sound less furious
than he was. 'But anyone beating a
child like that is the business of any
decent human being. The boy's had
more than enough.'

'That's for me to decide,' the man
declared.

Even as he spoke he dived from his
kneeling position at Sam, as swift as a
striking rattlesnake. Instead of backing
away or dodging, Sam stepped
forward, lifting a knee into the face
that hurtled toward him. It connected

with a crunching jar.

The force of the blow lifted the big man nearly upright. Sam stepped in right behind it with a powerful right to the man's stomach. His breath deserted him in a loud huff.

Without waiting, Sam began systematically venting his outrage with his fists. He alternated sharp blows that ripped and bruised the man's face with crushing body blows, each of which either broke or cracked a rib.

In minutes, the big man's face was a shapeless mass of bloody tissue. His arms hung uselessly at his sides. He hunched slightly forward, swaying back and forth.

Sam stepped back and eyed his handiwork critically, as an artist might survey his canvas. Satisfied, he sent an overhand right into the man's chin. He fell backward like an axed tree, and lay spread-eagled where he landed.

Without wasting another look at his defeated adversary, Sam turned to tend to the boy. He blinked in surprise. The lad was nowhere to be seen. He looked all around, and finally called, 'Where'd you go, son? You better let me take a look at you. Might be we'd oughta take you to the doctor.'

There was no response. Sam looked around at the houses that lay within his vision. He reasoned the man and boy probably lived in one of them, but there should have been some kind of response from the other houses that lay within sight and sound. Surely their residents couldn't have been oblivious to what had occurred, both before and after Sam's arrival.

Even so, there was nothing. Not one face in a window; not one neighbor venturing out to speak; not one concerned citizen of Big Springs that cared to get involved.

Frowning, Sam wiped the blood from his hands on the unconscious man's shirt, then resumed his way toward the Lucky Drover.

In front of the saloon he stopped and dunked his hands in the water trough beneath the hitch rail. The cool water felt good. He cringed as he watched the water turn red. It didn't bother him that his knuckles were bloodied. It suddenly bothered him that he was bloodying the water the horses would have to drink.

The street seemed strangely empty, except for the apparently drunk cowboy slouched on the bench in front of the saloon. His hat was down over his eyes, and Sam couldn't tell if he was conscious or not. He shook his hands free of the water, examined his knuckles briefly, then walked on into the saloon.

'Whiskey,' he told the bartender, tossing a coin onto the bar.

The bartender set a shot glass in front of him and filled it. He glanced briefly at Sam's knuckles, then pushed the coin back. 'This one's on the house.'

Sam's eyebrows rose. 'How's come?'

'Anybody that messes up his knuckles that bad on Gar Newberry deserves one.'

'Is that his name? How'd you know about that already?'

The bartender shrugged. 'Small town. I heard you laced him out plumb good.'

'He was beatin' the livin' daylights out've a little kid.'

'Tad.'

'What?'

'Tad. The kid's name's Tad. He's Gar's kid.'

'He beat him like that regular?'

The bartender shrugged again. 'Not usually that bad, but yeah. He's plumb hard on the kid. Always has been, I reckon, but worse since the boy's ma disappeared.'

'Disappeared?'

'Run off, most likely. Got tired o' bein' beat on.'

'Sounds like this guy has a habit o' beatin' up on women and kids. Why hasn't somebody put a stop to it?'

The bartender hesitated a long moment. Finally he said, 'It ain't generally considered too healthy a thing to cross Newberry.'

'The whole town's scared of 'im?'

'Somethin' like that, I guess. And you didn't hear it from me. If anybody asks, I never had this here conversation, and I sure didn't buy you no drink. But watch your back.'

He turned and moved away, clearly finished with the conversation. Sam took a small sip of the whiskey and set it down on the bar. He turned his back to the bar, hooked the heel of one boot on the brass rail, and surveyed the interior of the saloon.

He had no sooner done so than a barrel-chested man stood up from a table next to the wall and bow-legged his way over to him. Without preamble he said, 'You a cowpoke?'

'Yup.'

'Are you any good?'

'Better'n most. I work hard. I ride for the brand. I treat horses right and handle the cows as gentle as I can. And I eat enough for three men.'

The rancher chuckled. 'Are you lookin' for work?'

'Yup.'

The man extended a hand. 'My name's Mort Halverson. My spread's the Circle T, about fifteen miles outa town. I could use a good man.'

'Any reason a hand wouldn't want to ride for you?'

Halverson blinked a couple times, his mouth hanging open. Then he grinned broadly. 'Well, now, that's a new one. Nobody's ever asked me that one.'

When he still didn't answer the question, Sam said, 'Well? Is there?'

Halverson's grin broadened. 'Well, now, I'm thinkin'. I do expect a day's work for a day's pay. I expect a man to ride for the brand. I don't put up with 'im abusin' my stock, horses or cows either one. But you already covered most o' that. Aside from that, I guess I'm just about the most wonderful man to work for that ever set foot in Wyoming Territory. Not to mention the best lookin', by a dang sight.'

Sam relaxed and returned the man's infectious grin. 'Now I don't know what more a man could ask for than that.'

A voice from the table where Halverson had been sitting spoke across the room. 'You don't wanta take that good-lookin' part serious. If he's the best lookin' rancher in the country, that'd make the rest of us uglier'n warts on a sick toad.'

Several laughed at the rancher's expense, then all turned back to their own conversations. 'Be at the livery barn at sunup,' Halverson said. 'I'll be headin' out with a buckboard full o' supplies. How many horses you got?'

'Two.'

The rancher nodded. 'You can tie 'em on behind and ride with me. We'll talk while we're on the way out home.'

He turned and went back to his friends. Sam tossed off the rest of his drink and walked back to the hotel. Well, at least he had a job. Maybe that was a start. Maybe. Or maybe he'd just made one enemy too many.

5

Life and death situations are never scheduled and marked on the calendar. In fact, they most often seem to show up when everything is supposed to be routine and uneventful.

Every hand on every ranch across the West saddled up every morning knowing the day might hold such an event. Never mind whether it was scheduled.

Sam had been working on the Circle T for a couple weeks, and liked the place. The only thing that bothered him was something he could only vaguely sense, never see or hear. It was as if some great cloud followed him, that threatened him in some indefinable way. Nobody else seemed aware of it. Nobody mentioned it. Nobody sensed it but Sam, but it seemed to grow, day by day.

An even greater sense of foreboding

had dogged Sam since he wakened this morning. It might have come from any number of sources. Bunkhouse talk most nights the past two weeks had been dominated by Ephraim Harris, the hand they all knew, who was hanged at his campsite by Broken Spoke Creek. The crew, most of whom had known him for several years, were unanimous that he would never have been involved in any holdup, let alone a cold-blooded murder. They were at a loss to explain the presence of the damning necklace in his saddle-bag. They all knew Johnny O'Neal, and understood his fervor to avenge his daughter's death, but they were convinced he had been wrong.

Sam's sense of impending danger was probably heightened by the crew's reaction to his own fight with Gar Newberry. Everybody knew him as a bully who never forgot a grudge.

Gossip had whispered word of Ephraim's confrontation with New-berry in Big Springs, the day before he was hanged. One hand dared to suggest that if he could figure out how he could have done so, he'd think it was Newberry who had planted the necklace in Ephraim's saddle-bag. Several nodded heads indicated other hands thought the man perfectly capable of such an act.

Though not a man among them would have admitted it, there was more than a trace of fear in every one of them as they mentioned his name. Several cautioned Sam to watch his back. They were just as unanimous in heartily approving the beating he had delivered to the universally disliked man.

In the course of one conversation, Sam mentioned the mystery of the young boy's disappearance. He was still puzzled that he could get out of sight so quickly and silently.

There was an awkward pause, as if everyone but Sam was privy to some bit of information they were all either embarrassed by, or a little fearful of because they knew it. Finally, Lennie

Lewis said, 'He likely lit out for Black Betty's.'

'Who's Black Betty?' Sam queried instantly.

'Was there a black whore in the Lucky Drover when you was there?'

Sam was silent, trying to remember who everyone was in the saloon. After a few moments his eyes lit up. 'Yeah! There was. She was standin' at the back end o' the bar, right by the back door, when I went in. What's she got to do with it?'

'She's sorta been lookin' after the kid from time to time, when things get too tough for him at home. Folks figure she lets him sleep in her room when he needs to, but everyone's careful not to know about it. No sense causin' her to get hurt.'

That would explain how everyone in the saloon knew about his beating of Newberry before he had arrived there. He frowned, looking around the bunkhouse to see if any face bore any indication that he was being strung along. He could detect no such hint. Finally he said, 'Newberry'd hurt her for helpin' his kid?'

'Helpin' the kid would mean goin' against Newberry. It ain't generally considered the healthiest thing in the world to cross Gar Newberry.'

Sam went to sleep that night wondering how long it would be before the big man felt healed enough to look for revenge. It had been two weeks. It was probably time for things to start going bad.

It was no real surprise, then, when the next day began to turn sour, right from the get-go.

Choosing to let his own horses rest for a few days, Sam saddled one of the ranch horses. As was normal, he had been given a string of ranch mounts to use as long as he worked on the Circle T. They were all good horses. He had picked for his mount of the day a big piebald mare. He stepped into the saddle. Predictably, the horse crow-hopped a few jumps around the corral, getting the kinks out, sizing up her new rider. Suddenly the cinch strap broke. Saddle and rider together shot airborne. Still solidly in the saddle, Sam found himself sitting on the ground with a bone-jarring thud.

'Hey, Sam,' a hand shouted immediately from the other side of the corral. 'Don't look now, but you lost your horse!'

Sam climbed off the saddle and made a big show of bending over and looking under the saddle. He straightened up and looked all around the corral. 'Where'd she go? She was under that saddle a minute ago.'

Several hands laughed, demonstrating the beginning of a bond that was essential to survival in the rugged life of the West. In just two weeks, Sam had become one of them.

Ed Runner, foreman of the Circle T, hollered, 'You'd best just grab one o' the ranch saddles outa the barn. You can fix yours after you come in tonight.'

Sam recognized the wisdom of the

foreman's orders. If he repaired his saddle before he started the day, the rest of the crew would be long gone. New to the ranch, he didn't know the country well enough to catch up with them. No matter what happened, he would be no help to the crew for at least half a day.

The saddle he picked from the rack in the barn didn't fit him badly, but it wasn't his saddle. The piebald mare wasn't his horse. He was just uncomfortable.

We are, all of us, creatures of habit. When our routines are unbroken, we're comfortable. When they're not, we're not. Have a man shave with the 'wrong' hand some morning, then watch as he struggles with a feeling of 'something's just not right,' for the whole day.

A cinch strap breaking was no big thing, but Sam was jolted out of his comfort zone. He didn't like the feeling. It just heightened in him that vague, nagging sense of unease.

Some small voice in the back of his

mind assured him that when a day starts off bad, it almost always goes downhill from there. His mood must have showed. Cap Baker rode up beside him half a mile from the ranch. 'Don't look so down-in-the-mouth, son,' he advised. 'Things could be worse.'

Sam looked at the weathered old cowpoke for whom he had felt an instant liking from his first day on the job. He grinned. 'Yeah, that's what worries me,' he said. 'One time a fella told me, 'Cheer up, son, things could be worse.' So I cheered up, and sure enough, things got worse.'

Cap chuckled. 'Some days are like that, all right. Where'd you hail from, Sam?'

'Nebraska.'

'Is that so? I rode for an outfit in Nebraska once. The Bartlett ranch, up in the panhandle.'

Sam nodded. 'I rode for the March-ants, a little ways west o' Bartlett's.'

'Is that so?' the old man repeated. 'Small world.'

He started to say something else, then broke it off and said, 'Watch it!' instead.

Sam's attention jerked in the direction of the older man's gaze. A shadow of movement in the edge of the timber was gone before he could identify it. 'What was that?'

'Lion.'

Sam relaxed slightly. 'Oh. He ain't likely to bother us, is he?'

'Not us, but Lennie's ridin' a green mare. She's kinda skittish. She might blow up.'

As Sam shifted his gaze to the young cowboy, he noted how tightly he was holding the mare's reins. Her ears were back flat against her head. Her nostrils flared. Her eyes rolled wildly. She pranced and danced, fighting against the reins. Lennie was bent as far forward as possible, talking into her ear as soothingly as he could. Even as he spoke, the mare surrendered to the panic that the smell and sight of the mountain lion engendered.

The terrified horse squealed and jumped sideways. She began to buck as if her rider were the lion, and her life depended on unseating him. Bent forward, trying to soothe the animal, Lennie wasn't ready for the sudden explosion of his mount. He slewed over to one side at the first jump, grabbing wildly for the saddle horn. The horse felt his weight shift, so her next jump was a wild sun-fishing leap in the opposite direction. Lennie was flung from the saddle, but his boot slid through the stirrup as he left his seat. Hung up by that foot, his life was suddenly in grave and immediate danger.

Sam and Cap were both already moving. Both had already grabbed their lariats and shaken out loops. They slammed spurs to the sides of their horses, equally frantic to get a rope on Lennie's terrified mount before her panicked plunging resulted in his being kicked in the head or dragged to death.

Sam started the second swing of the

loop of his lariat around his head when it happened. Maybe the piebald's front foot stepped in a hole. Maybe a hoof caught on the root of something. Maybe it just folded up under her. Whatever the reason, she went down hard. Sam shot over her head, somersaulted in the air, and struck the ground just as hard, flat on his back. Inevitably, it being the day it was, he landed in a patch of flat-leafed cactus, bristling with two-inch spines.

Faring better than Sam, Cap cast his loop and watched it descend over the head of Lennie's fleeing mare. Just as it did, a hard jerk on the rope secured the loop around the animal's neck. Taking a quick dally around his saddle horn, Cap leaped from the saddle and hit the ground running.

As the rope tightened, Cap's horse set his feet and leaned back against the anticipated pull on the lariat. The force of the tether brought the mare up short and forced her to whirl toward the sudden restraint. Another cowboy beat

Cap to the frightened mount. He, too, leaped from his horse and grabbed Lennie's foot and the stirrup, twisting the stirrup upward so the cowboy's foot fell free.

As three ranch-hands held and calmed the terrified horse, Lennie rolled over and struggled to his feet. He took a quick step sideways to keep from falling.

'You OK?' Cap demanded.

'I'm fine,' Lennie responded instantly.

Every eye watched him critically, knowing that every cowboy, if he is capable of crawling or walking, instinctively says either, 'I'm OK,' or 'I'm fine.' He may pass out, or even die from his injuries almost at once, but he will certainly assure all who are there that he's 'fine' before he does.

'I think he's better off than the new fella,' another cowboy observed.

All eyes turned toward Sam. He had struggled out of the cactus patch, and was bent over, pulling out the long cactus spines one at a time. His jaw was clamped. His brow was pulled down until his eyes were mere slits. Two of the crew walked over and silently began to help him remove the cactus stickers, especially from his backside where his chaps offered no protection and he couldn't reach very well.

Ed, the ranch foreman, stalked over and faced Sam, hands on hips. 'I don't know whether we're gonna be able to keep you on or not,' he remonstrated in a severe tone of voice. 'First you bust your cinch strap so you gotta use one o' our saddles, then you send one of the boss's horses head over teakettle, and now you go and bust off all the stickers from one o' the best cactus patches we got on the place. Where do you think an old steer's gonna find to scratch his butt if you bust off all the cactus?'

With a perfectly straight face Sam said, 'I'm tryin' my best to pull 'em all out without bustin' any. I was sure you'd wanta put 'em all back where they was.'

'You busted 'em off, you put 'em

back,' the foreman retorted with feigned anger.

The crew stood around and traded small talk until all the stickers had been removed that could be. Everybody knew that several of the sharp spines had inevitably broken off. Those few would fester. When they did, they could possibly be accessed with the tip of a knife, then squeezed. If they were properly festered, the offending sticker would pop out and the irritating wound would begin to heal. Again, it was no big deal, but Sam knew he had a week of pretty severe discomfort to look forward to. Besides, every spot there had been a cactus spine stung like fire from whatever poison the plant secreted on its thorns.

He went to his horse and lifted her front leg, carefully checking her. Her left ankle was already beginning to swell. He led her in a wide circle, watching her favor the tender leg. It was instantly obvious that he wasn't going to be able to ride her.

The foreman hollered at Baker. 'Cap, you got your big gelding today. You and Sam can ride double and lead the mare back to the place.'

Cap nodded. 'You want us to catch up with you boys, then?'

Ed shook his head. 'No, we'll be six or eight miles ahead of you by the time you get back to the place and catch up another horse. Naw, why don't you two ride on over and check on the bulls in that south pasture. That low draw was lookin' the other day like it might get boggy. I don't want any o' them high-priced bulls the boss went and bought gettin' bogged down.'

Cap nodded. 'That'll keep us outa trouble most o' the day.'

Ed grinned. 'Or get you into trouble, if you have to drag a mad bull out've a bog, then try to get your ropes off'n him again.'

With a perfectly straight face Cap said, 'Aw, we'll just likely leave our ropes on 'im and let Mort buy us new ones.'

'I'll tell Mort your idea.'

'No, you tell him that part was Sam's idea. I like my job.'

'Hey now!' Sam protested, 'How'd I get into this?'

'By bustin' your cinch, lamin' your horse, and usin' up all my crew's time pullin' stickers outa your hind side, that's how.'

Without answering, Sam fashioned a halter and lead rope out of his lariat and put it on the mare. He swung up behind Cap on the gelding, and the two headed for the ranch at a trot.

Cap's big Morgan gelding was a magnificent animal. He carried the double weight with no apparent effort. The pair was just over a mile from the Circle T ranch headquarters when Sam and Cap simultaneously caught a brief flash of reflected sunlight.

'Look out!' both yelled at exactly the same time. As they yelled, both were already moving, diving from the gelding. Each man tucked a shoulder, hit the ground, and rolled.

Sam leaped to his feet, lunged to his mare, and jerked his rifle from the saddle scabbard. In the same continuous motion he dived away from the mare, headfirst behind a large clump of brush. As he dived, he heard Cap's rifle bark. He rolled to one knee and brought the rifle to his shoulder, pointing it at the exact spot where he had seen the flash of light. His rifle roared as the stock hit his shoulder.

He instantly lunged sideways and took shelter behind a large pine tree. Its lowest branches were five feet from the ground, allowing him to peer around the huge trunk.

'Did ya see 'im?' he asked softly.

'Nope,' Cap answered instantly. 'You OK?'

'Yeah. He was close enough I heard the slug buzz past.'

'Pertnear got you, huh?'

'Way too close, for sure. You got a good view of where he's at?'

'Can't see 'im, but I can see the spot he's gotta be holed up in.'

'Keep 'im busy. I'll see if I can circle around.'

'There's a shallow draw 'bout a hundred feet to your right. If you follow it, it'll lead you right around behind him.'

'Sounds perfect.'

'Too perfect. Two to one he'll figure that's what you're doin', and be layin' for you there.'

Sam mulled over the information. 'I'll leave the draw about halfway there, then. There's pretty heavy timber over there. I might be able to out-guess 'im and sneak up on 'im.'

Worming his way backward, straight away from the tree that provided his cover, Sam worked his way past a thick stand of plum bushes. Using them for cover, he scurried toward the draw Cap had suggested. It was perfect for his purpose. Wide and shallow, the bottom was kept relatively free of vegetation by the fast water that always followed summer thunder showers. He could nearly run, his steps muffled by the lush grass.

An occasional rifle shot attested to Cap's effort to keep their attacker pinned down. Whether it would work or not remained to be seen.

When he thought he should be about halfway to the bushwhacker, he carefully made his way up the side of the draw. The timber around him was dense, allowing vision for only short distances. Walking with as near total silence as he could manage in riding boots, he advanced from tree to tree, trying not to expose himself more than absolutely necessary.

He worked his way to where he thought the ideal spot for another ambush should be located. As he moved from one tree to another, he caught a small flash of movement from ahead of his location, closer to the draw. His rifle leaped to his shoulder and fired in one lightning move.

He was rewarded with a sudden curse and the sound of crashing brush.

He could follow the sound of someone fleeing recklessly for nearly three minutes. Abrupt silence for a few seconds was then followed by the sounds of a horse running headlong for open country.

Cap's voice floated through the trees. 'Don't sound like you slowed him down a whole lot.'

'I ain't sure I hit 'im at all,' Sam confessed. 'Just caught a glimpse of 'im.'

'You either hit 'im or come plumb awful close,' Cap assured him. 'A man don't usually yell like that unless it's one or the other.'

'Ain't much sense tryin' to chase 'im.'

'Naw. He's long gone, and us with one good horse betwixt us. Ain't much doubt who it was, though.'

Sam walked back to where Cap waited with the horses. As he emerged from the timber, he tripped on a rock and nearly fell. Lunging to catch his balance, he took a long step. As his boot struck the ground, the heel caught on the tip of another rock. It jerked his foot from beneath him, sending him sprawling on the ground.

He leaped to his feet, wishing for all he was worth that Cap wasn't standing there grinning from ear to ear, watching his unaccustomed clumsiness. With the first step he nearly fell again. Only then did he realize he had broken the heel off his boot. He turned back and found it, lying in the grass. He limped to the horses, carrying the boot heel, hoping against hope that Cap wouldn't say anything.

He might just as well wish the moon would cross the sky backward. Cap's dry voice betrayed no trace of humor. 'You know, there's some days a fella just shouldn't get outa bed.'

'You sure you want me ridin' double with you?' Sam asked. 'I might bust your horse's back, the way this day is goin'.'

Instead of answering, Cap said, 'Hank's got boot lasts in his blacksmith shop at the ranch. He can have your boot fixed whilst we're gettin' you a different horse saddled. That and eatin' dinner. It's gonna be close enough to noon that Cookie'll have some dinner ready.'

'You 'spect I can eat it without chokin' today?'

'I ain't layin' any money on you today atall.'

Sam did manage to eat the satisfying meal without incident. He caught up another horse without breaking a leg and his boot heel was repaired, just as good as new. Maybe he'd not only survived, but outlasted his streak of bad luck.

Hours later the pair rode back into the Circle T ranch yard. 'Well, we made it home in one piece,' Cap's dry voice observed.

'It's what I call a good day,' Sam agreed. 'We didn't find any bulls bogged down, didn't get attacked by any mad bear, and didn't see even one hydrophoby skunk.'

'Not to mention, we got missed by the only guy that bothered to shoot at us all day.'

'Yeah. Not to mention that.'

6

Sam squirmed, leaning over to one side, gripping the curved rod at the end of the seat of the bouncing buckboard. 'I swear a saddle would hurt less than this buckboard seat.'

Cy Reeves chuckled. 'There ain't no way to sit that hurts any less, when you land in a cactus patch like that. You gonna let the doctor take a look at you whilst we're in town?'

'Yeah, I 'spect.'

Cy nodded. 'I 'spect you better, anyhow. I'd lay you two to one that the boss's wife is the one that thought o' you goin' to town with me today, just so you could do that without havin' to ask for the time off.'

Sam turned bright red. 'She knows about it?'

Cy laughed. 'Hey, you're the funniest thing that happened on the Circle T

70

since that ol' grizzly sow kept Al Summers up a tree for two days. You don't think there's any way Mort ain't gonna share it with his wife, do you?'

Sam swore. 'Now I'm gonna think about that every time I see her.'

Cy laughed again, reveling in the younger man's discomfiture. 'Ain't no way around it,' he assured Sam. 'O' course, she won't say nothin'.'

'She won't need to.'

'Aw, you'll feel better about it after Doc gets the festered-up stickers outa ya.'

'I hope so. I'd try to ride this danged contraption standin' up, but the way my luck's been runnin' lately, I'd fall over the side and break my neck.'

'You've sure enough had a bad run o' luck all right. Reminds me o' the winter of sixty-two, when me an' old Clint Hobbs was . . . '

For the rest of the way to town the old flunkee rambled on, oblivious to the fact that Sam had long since stopped listening.

Cy drove the buckboard directly to the building that boasted a sign advertising 'Dr Silas Stringwell, MD,' with an arrow pointing up the narrow outside stairs. Sam climbed painfully down, relieved in spite of the pain, just to be no longer sitting. 'I'll be down at the Mercantile Store, loadin' up the supplies,' Cy advised.

Nodding wordlessly, Sam walked up the long stairway and opened the door. To his dismay, a pretty young lady sat behind a desk. She looked up as he entered. 'Good morning. Can I help you?'

Sam felt his face flush crimson. 'I, uh, that is, uh, well, uh, is the doc in?'

'Yes he is. May I tell him the nature of your complaint?'

Sam knew his face took on an even deeper shade of red, but he couldn't help that any more than he could help his ability to talk without stuttering. 'Uh, well, that is, I, uh, I got a bunch o' cactus stickers in me that I can't get out.'

Her eyes danced at his embarrassment, but she refrained from making any comment. She nodded toward a leather divan. 'Just have a seat, and I'll tell Doctor Stringwell you're here.'

As soon as she said it, she noticed the pained expression that crossed his face. She couldn't help adding, with her eyes still dancing, 'Or you're welcome to stand up while you wait if that's more comfortable.'

She didn't stay to watch his face color turn more than its already impossible shade of red. She disappeared into a hallway, reappearing moments later. 'Right this way, Mr — ?'

'Uh, Murray. Sam.'

'Right this way, Sam. Doctor Stringwell is right in there.'

He hurried to the door she indicated and ducked out of sight, closing it quickly behind himself. It was nearly an hour later when he walked out again. The removal of all the festered stickers and whatever balm the doctor had applied helped tremendously. So had whatever was in that elixir. The doctor gave him a large spoonful of some bitter liquid before he started working on the stickers. In moments his head was swimming slightly, but the pain was remarkably less. As he walked back out, he noted three other people waiting to see the doctor. The girl behind the desk said, 'That will be two dollars, Mr Murray. If you have it.'

He stopped in sudden surprise. He had never been to a doctor before. It hadn't occurred to him that it cost money. As soon as he realized, he felt like a total fool. Of course doctors had to be paid! They needed to make a living like everybody else.

He fished two dollars out of his pocket and handed them to the girl. 'Do you feel better?' she couldn't resist asking.

He knew his face turned crimson again, but he just smiled. 'A whole bunch better, thanks.'

Then, not believing he heard himself

saying it, he said, 'At least he didn't ask you to help.'

She giggled. 'As embarrassed as you were, I think you'd have left with the stickers all firmly in place.'

He started to answer, but he had already expended the supply of bravado that the spoon of bitter liquid had supplied along with its pain-relieving qualities. 'Yes, ma'am,' he mumbled as he walked out.

He walked to the Cross Mercantile Store, feeling almost euphoric. As he entered the store, a bright, cheerful voice said, 'Good morning! Can I help you?'

A middle-aged, slightly built woman stood behind a counter, smiling at him. Her hair was pulled back in a bun, gray streaks showing along the sides. He liked her at once. 'Is Cy Reeves here? He's supposed to be gettin' some stuff for the Circle T.'

She nodded. 'My husband is helping him load the buckboard at the loading dock out back. I'm Lila Cross. I don't think I've met you.'

As she spoke she thrust her hand out across the counter. He took the hand and returned the strong, almost masculine grip. 'I'm Sam Murray. I just hired on at the Circle T a while back.'

Her eyes lit up with instant recognition. 'Ah! You're the one that, uh, confronted our town bully, I hear.'

At a loss for words, he mumbled something unintelligible.

She seemed not to notice. 'Sam. Is that short for Samuel? Like the prophet?'

'Uh, no. No, it's Sylvester.'

'Sylvester! My! How does one get Sam out of that?'

He smiled at her audacity. 'It's actually my initials. My folks gave me one of them long handles that takes half a day and two drinks of water to say, so it got shortened down some.'

'I see. What is your full name?'

Sounding as if he were mouthing somebody else's difficult name, he replied, 'Sylvester Anthony Murray. The initials spell out Sam, so that's a whole bunch easier.'

'My, that is a mouthful, all right. But it's a strong and distinguished name. I should think you'd like it.'

When he couldn't think of an answer, she pointed toward the back of the store. 'You're welcome to go out and help them finish loading, unless you're needing some things for yourself.'

'Uh, no. I guess not. Not today.'

He hurried through the door, not at all sure why he was so bashful in the presence of anyone wearing a dress today. He helped Cy and Lester Cross load the last of the supplies then he and Cy roped down the buckboard's contents to keep anything from jostling out on the road home. When they had finished Cy said, 'Wanta stop an' wet our whistles afore we head back?'

'Sure. Does the Lucky Drover have sandwiches an' such?'

'Yup. Nothin' real special, but it'll keep our belly buttons from rubbin' on our backbones till we get home. There's a pretty good café, too, but you gotta pay for the grub there, and you don't get a beer with it either.'

They tied the team and wagon in front of the saloon and walked inside. It was cool and dark in the interior. They paused just inside the door to let their eyes accustom. Sam spotted him at once.

Gar Newberry leaned on the bar, two-thirds of the way toward the back of the saloon. He had a beer in front of him. A dirty white rag was tied around his head. It showed a spot of blood that had seeped through at the top of the ear. His face still bore marks from the beating Sam had given him, though the bruising had lost most of its color. Instead of the deep purple, they were a pale yellow, with hints of green in spots. Enough of the swelling had subsided that his face was nearly normal.

When he spotted Sam he stood up straight, one hand still on the bar. It was apparent from his action that his ribs were far from healed, and that he was otherwise still stiff and sore. He eyed Sam with a malevolent glare, but said nothing.

Sam felt the hairs on the back of his neck raise. He remembered the whine of the bullet that had nearly got him as he and Cap had dived from the horse's back. He remembered the yell and curse that followed his own shot directed toward their bushwhacker. The bandage on Gar's head might well be the result of that shot's catching the tip of his ear.

Sam's hand brushed against his gun butt. 'Been doin' some ridin' lately, Newberry?' he demanded.

Newberry shook his head. 'Ain't exactly felt like ridin' lately.'

'What happened to your ear?'

'Now I don't see as how that's any o' your business.'

'It just might be. Somebody took a shot at me a couple days or so ago. I think I mighta clipped him a little bit. What happened to your ear?'

The bartender appeared to be trying

to hide a grin, but he said nothing. Sam couldn't decide whether something funny had happened to Newberry, or he was amused that someone was on the attack against the man most of the town was afraid of.

Finally, Newberry said, 'If it's any o' your business, I grabbed a cat by the tail when it tried to walk into my house. I hate cats. When I went to whirl him around my head to heave him out into the street, he went an' took off a piece o' my ear on the way by.'

It sounded a little preposterous. On the other hand, what proof did he have that it wasn't true? At least that seemed to be the version the bartender had heard as well. That accounted for his amusement. Even so, it seemed too big a coincidence to be probable.

At the same time, the story was too degrading for the town bully to be telling it if it wasn't the truth. Besides, Newberry's movements seemed pretty stiff and slow for him to be riding that far, or moving as fast as Sam's attacker had moved. Adrenaline can compensate for a lot of discomfort, though. So can hatred, and Sam knew the man hated him passionately.

Deciding he didn't have enough proof to press the issue, Sam turned his attention to the bartender. He carefully kept an eye on Newberry, even as he spoke. 'How about a couple beers and sandwiches?'

'Sure thing,' the bartender agreed.

He delivered the beers first, then made the sandwiches and placed them in front of them on surprisingly clean plates. He took Sam's money for the beers. 'Sandwiches are on the house,' he explained.

'That so?' Sam queried, as if he hadn't already known that from Cy.

The bartender's face was expressionless. 'Yeah, we give the lunch away. Then we put lots o' salt on it, so you'll get good and thirsty. Then you'll order another beer.'

'Yeah, but when I drink more'n one beer, I always get hungry.'

'Then I'll make you another free sandwich. Real salty. You boys may be here all day.'

Snorting loudly at the less-than-funny exchange, Newberry pushed away from the bar and made his way out the door, walking carefully.

'He still seems a bit stove up,' Cy noted.

The bartender grinned openly, now that Newberry was gone. 'He ain't bad, now. You shoulda seen 'im when he first got whupped up on. Doc hadta take care of 'im at home for pertnear a week, afore he could get up and around. He's just now gettin' his normal nasty disposition back.'

'I shoulda kept workin' on 'im a little longer,' Sam opined. 'Maybe I coulda beat it all out've 'im.'

The bartender shook his head. 'You'd have had to kill 'im to do that.'

'Yeah, I 'spect. Is his kid OK?'

'Seems to be. As OK as he has a chance to be.'

'Too bad a kid has to live with that.'

'Just don't forget to watch your back,' the bartender reminded him. 'You ain't likely heard the last from Gar.'

Sam nodded, still not convinced he hadn't already been the target of the man's intended revenge. He sure didn't know who else in this country might try to kill him from ambush. He'd been around less than a month.

Sometimes, it doesn't take a man long to be noticed.

It was just that unreasonable caution that caused him to mutter to Cy, 'Who's the cowpoke at the far table?'

Without turning to look, Cy spoke back just as softly, 'Felix Walker.'

'He ride for one of the outfits around?'

'Nah. He can't seem to stay sober long enough to ride for nobody. He just hangs around town.'

'What's he live on?'

'Millie.'

'Who's Millie?'

'One o' the whores that works here. She's got a crib upstairs, but she actually lives in a house down the street. Felix lives with her.'

'Now why would a woman, even a whore, support a drunk that won't work?'

Cy shrugged. 'Believe it or not, I asked her that once. She said, 'Everybody looks down on us whores, like we're the scum o' the earth. I need somebody around that I can look down on.''

Sam grunted.

'Or, it could be,' Cy continued, 'that she actually loves the guy.'

Sam shook his head. 'Seems strange that a woman could love a man she doesn't respect.'

'Love is always strange, Sam. There ain't no way to understand it.'

That was true for more things than love, Sam had already learned.

7

The yell came just as the stagecoach reached the top of Tugman Hill. Shorty Whitcomb yelled, 'Whoooaaa!'

Before the echo of his command to the horses bounced from the nearby cliffs, another voice yelled, 'Throw up your hands!'

Shorty released a single expletive as he shoved the stage's brake lever with his foot. The shotgun guard gripped his Greener, obviously weighing his chances. 'Don't even try it!' the masked gunman yelled. 'I'll get three slugs in ya before you can lift that thing.'

The guard recognized the better part of valor and tossed the shotgun over the side. Shorty wrapped the lines around the brake handle and raised his hands.

The gunman yelled at the passengers. 'Everybody out, one at a time, with your hands where I can see 'em. And don't nobody think you can sneak out the other side. I can see under the stage, and I'll shoot your feet off if you try it.'

The door of the coach flew open. One at a time the passengers began to climb out, keeping their hands in plain view. First came an apparent salesman with a rotund belly and red face. He looked furiously affronted, but held his peace.

Second came a strikingly beautiful young lady. Her coppery curls fell in ringlets from beneath a large sun bonnet. A smattering of freckles bridged her nose. Her eyes were a startling shade of green and her small mouth was drawn tight, making her look much more irritated than afraid. She kept her hands in plain sight, but refused to raise them above her head.

A matronly lady, who was probably pushing forty, followed her out. Her more than ample bosom was well secured with a corset that had to be intensely uncomfortable on the stage ride. Her dress covered her shoes and fashionably touched the ground. She carried a handbag large enough to pack a change of clothes, a dozen diapers, and the baby that wore them. She 'harrumphed' as she tugged at the bottom of her corset through her dress.

A weathered cowboy climbed out, chewing a match that jutted from one corner of his mouth. He looked more bemused than anything, as if he'd been in this situation before and probably would be again.

While the other passengers were disembarking from the Concord, a young cowboy quietly climbed out a window on the far side. Trying his best to do so silently, he found footholds on the side of the coach and crept toward the back. He hung on to the luggage boot and squirmed his way around to where he thought he could get a shot at the highwayman.

He was brave. He was foolish. He was young. He would grow no older.

Not thinking to remove his hat, it telegraphed his presence before he got into a position to see the robber. As if he were plinking at tin cans, the gunman shot him off the back of the stage as soon as his head came into view. The young man toppled to the ground, dead before he landed.

'Anybody else wanta play hero?' the masked gunman demanded.

Clearly, nobody did. He pointed a gun at the matronly woman. 'You. Grab a lap blanket outa the coach. And make sure that's all you try to grab.'

She glared as if to defy him. Her eyes darted to the dead man behind the coach. A red stain had already spread from beneath his head. Her face paled. She compressed her lips and turned back to the coach, coming back in seconds with a plaid wool robe.

'Spread it on the ground.'

She did so.

'Now, startin' with you. Dump that carpetbag onto the blanket.'

Her affront at having her handbag

called a carpetbag was instantly obvious. She shot another look at the dead cowboy, then complied. 'Now get back there with the others,' the man ordered.

One at a time he forced the passengers to relinquish their valuables. It appeared as if he would order them all back into the coach until the rifle barked.

★　★　★

'That was a shot.'

Sam Murray and Lennie Lewis reined in their horses.

'Right about the top o' Tugman Hill, sounds like,' Lennie agreed.

'C'mon!' Sam replied, slamming the spurs to his horse.

The pair lunged up the road, urging their horses to their utmost. As they crested the hill, Sam swung his mount sideways. The animal stopped dead still, as if reading his rider's mind.

Sam's eyes took in the scene in an instant. A masked man on foot, a little over three hundred yards away, held the passengers of the stagecoach at bay. A blanket lay on the ground between them. As the pair topped the hill, the outlaw was motioning with his pistol. Rifle already at his shoulder, Sam fired the instant his mount stopped. Lennie's rifle barked a second later.

Sam allowed perfectly for the distance, but not for the fact that his target was higher in elevation. His bullet kicked up dust just at the outlaw's feet. Lennie's shot, that second later, was twenty yards short of the target. Both riders levered a second round into the chambers of their rifles as quickly as they fired.

Sam's second shot was right on target, and would have brought the brigand down if his reflexes had been an instant slower. When Sam's bullet kicked up dust at his feet he wheeled and lunged backward, without taking time to spot his unexpected adversary. He never slowed. Ducking and dodging, he plunged into the brush and timber, out of sight.

Both Sam and Lennie sent a final round into the brush and trees, even though they both knew full well they had almost no chance whatever of finding their mark. At least it would prevent the man from turning around and returning fire from the cover of the brush.

Seconds later they heard the sound of a horse crashing its way through the thicket in headlong flight.

They both shoved their rifles into their saddle scabbards and kicked their mounts forward. As they approached, Sam's eyes riveted on the young woman. All the passengers had lowered their hands, recognizing that they had been rescued. The drummer was already picking through the booty on the blanket, sorting out his own valuables and reclaiming them.

Lennie leaped from his horse to examine the cowboy sprawled on the ground. A glance was all that was necessary to ascertain that he was dead.

The robber's bullet had entered just above the bridge of the man's nose and ripped away a large portion of the back of his skull as it exited. He had never felt his own death, nor known that his gallant effort had precipitated it.

Sam didn't notice. He knew he was staring, open-mouthed, at the young woman. He felt as if he were making a fool of himself, but neither cared nor was capable of stopping. It seemed as if his whole life had been hurtling toward this one moment when his eyes would meet hers, and his future, his hopes, his whole being was being swept into the bottomless depths of her sparkling eyes.

'Dear Lord, let her be single,' he prayed silently.

He stepped from his horse and walked toward her. 'Are you all right?' he asked.

'Yes, thanks to you,' she responded, staring back into his eyes with a gaze that seemed just as rapt as his own.

The matronly woman at the young lady's side harumphed loudly. 'Yes, thank you, young man. We are quite all right now.'

Her tone clearly indicated that Sam had been summarily dismissed. He ignored the matron completely. 'My name's Sam Murray,' Sam told the young lady.

The younger lady held out her hand. 'Hi. I'm Dorrie Birdwell.'

'I'm plumb awful glad to meet you,' Sam said.

'Ahem! And I am Cinderella Nelson,' the older lady intruded, holding out her own hand. 'You may call me Cindy. I am the wife of the saddle-maker in Big Springs, and also the school-teacher. School is dismissed for the summer at present, of course.'

Sam recovered his aplomb enough to acknowledge her. He took her hand and shook it, holding it not nearly as long as he had Dorrie's. 'Happy to meet you too, ma'am. Are you sure you're all right?'

'We are quite all right now, yes, thank you,' she responded.

Sam turned his attention back to

Dorrie instantly. 'Do you live in Big Springs?'

'About ten miles out. My folks have the Gadfly Ranch.'

'Gadfly,' Sam responded. 'Oh. The G Bar F?'

She smiled broadly, and Sam felt as if his knees were going to buckle. 'That's it. When they started out it was the GDF, but that's too hard to brand without it blotting, so I got left out.'

Sam frowned. 'You got left out?'

Her smile broadened. 'Yeah. My folks are Greta and Frank. They wanted the brand to be Greta, Dorene, Frank — GDF. But like I said, that blotted real bad. Then Daniel was born, so they couldn't have the whole family in the brand anyway, so they shortened it to G Bar F.'

'So you have a younger brother.'

'Two of them, actually. Daniel's just three years younger than me, and David is thirteen now.'

Suddenly remembering where he was and the circumstances, Sam forced himself to pay attention to his surroundings. The men from the stage, with Lennie's help, had lifted the dead cowboy's body onto the top of the stage. Everyone except Dorrie had recovered their valuables and climbed back into the coach. Sam and Dorrie were suddenly very conspicuous, standing together, apart from everyone else. Trying to mask his embarrassment, Sam motioned to the blanket, still lying on the ground. 'Uh, I 'spect you oughta get your stuff,' he suggested, nodding toward the blanket.

'Oh!' she said, equally embarrassed at the situation.

While she gathered her things, Sam walked toward the driver. 'Did you recognize the guy?'

Shorty's face bore an expression between sorrow and agony. 'Well, sorta. No, I don't have any idee who he is. None atall. But I'd swear he was the same guy that held us up afore.'

'The one that shot the woman, that I heard about?'

'Yup.'

The shotgun guard spoke up. 'But that'd mean them guys went an' hung the wrong man for that one.'

Shorty's reply was cryptic, but laden with emotion. 'Yup.'

'But they found some of the holdup stuff in his saddle-bag.'

'Yup.'

'So how'd it get there, if he wasn't the guy that held up the stage?'

'I don't have any idee. I did try to tell 'em he wasn't big enough. This here fella — the one that held us up then, and now again today — I'll swear it was the same guy — was pretty good sized. I did try to tell 'em. Really, I did.'

'But they didn't listen?'

After a long pause Shorty said, 'I don't guess any of us was none too anxious to listen. We seen the necklace. Johnny recognized it. We shoulda took 'im into town.'

'So you hung the wrong man?'

Shorty kicked at the dirt with the toe of his boot. He raised his head and stared off across country, above the tops of the trees, for a long moment. He took a deep, ragged breath. 'Yup. I reckon. That there ain't gonna be easy to live with. For any of us.'

He wheeled and strode to the stagecoach, climbing the wheel and on up to the seat. Sam turned back to Dorrie. The blanket had been picked up, so nothing remained on the ground. She stood at the door of the stage, watching him, clearly hoping he would say something more to her. He walked to her side and held out his hand to assist her into the stage. She stared into his eyes for a long moment, then took his hand. 'Can I see you again?' he heard himself unexpectedly ask her as she started to step up.

She stopped instantly, one foot up on the edge of the coach's floor. 'I was hoping you would,' she said softly. 'Do you know where the ranch is?'

'If I didn't, you can bet your last dollar I'd find it,' he grinned.

She smiled back at him and climbed

into the coach. The glow of that smile radiated through and through him. He stood motionless, holding the reins of his horse, until the stagecoach was long out of sight. Finally Lennie said, 'You gonna stop starin' after her an' remember what we're supposed to be doin' after a while?'

With a start, Sam brought himself back from the fantasies playing through his mind. He took a deep breath and let it out slowly. 'Yeah, if I hafta,' he said.

8

'I'm tellin' you it had to be Newberry.'

'I don't know. Gar's a bully. He rubs me the wrong way, same as he does everybody. But I don't think he's sneaky enough to do that there.'

Half a dozen ranchers were sitting around a table in the Lucky Drover, debating the identity of the stage robber. Because of the second robbery, and Shorty Whitcomb's insistence that it was the same highwayman, they had come to the somber conclusion that the young cowboy had been framed.

Johnny O'Neal joined the conversation briefly, but he couldn't deal with it long. He hadn't been sober since the night of the lynching. Added to the loss of his wife and daughter was the knowledge that he had personally executed an innocent man.

He had set out to be part of the

ranchers' conversation, but had soon retired alone to the corner table where he drank himself into a complete stupor every night.

'Eff was a light sleeper,' Mort Halverson said. 'I can't see Newberry bein' able to sneak into his camp and put nothin' into his saddle-bag without waking him up.'

'So who was it?'

'If I knew that, I'd be shag-tailin' after 'im, insteada sittin here chinnin' with you boys.'

Paul Endicott, owner of another ranch, spoke up. 'I heard tell Newberry did ride into town just a ways ahead o' the stage. His horse was all lathered up, like he'd run 'im a ways. He'da had plenty o' time to get to town ahead o' the stage.'

'Felix said Newberry picked a fight with Harris, too. Over a spot at the hitch rail. He went for his gun, and Eff stuck his own gun under Newberry's nose and made 'im back down.'

Frank Birdwell snorted. 'Now how

would Felix know? He's either dead drunk, on his way to bein' dead drunk, or just soberin' up with the shakes just about all the time.'

'Yeah, but I ain't sure he's always as drunk as everyone thinks. He sure seems to know everything that goes on in town.'

'He should. His rear end's pertnear growed to that bench out front. It or the sidewalk, 'cause he's too drunk to stay on the bench without slidin' off.'

'Anyhow, I don't think there's any way Eff coulda beat Newberry to the draw. That guy's greased lightnin'.'

'Why do you s'pose Gar would pick a fight over that in the first place?'

Several sets of shoulders shrugged in an almost synchronized motion. ''Cause he's Gar,' somebody finally said.

'Or to make sure everyone knew he was in town afore the stage came in,' Endicott argued.

The others stared at Paul Endicott a long moment. It was Mort that said, 'Are you sayin' you think Gar Newberry held up the stage, raced back to town to beat it here, picked a fight with Eff so's everyone would know he was here when the stage came in, then followed Eff out to where he camped, snuck into his camp and put that there necklace in his saddle-bag, then come back to town and led the rest out to where Eff was camped?'

There was another long silence. Finally Paul said, 'It does sound a bit far-fetched, don't it?'

Frank Birdwell said, 'There ain't none of it that I'd put past Newberry, if I could figure out how he did it. But it does seem a stretch to think he could do it.'

'Well, it don't look like there's any outa-work hands hangin' around waitin' for somebody to get their stuff outa hock today, so I gotta get home,' Paul said, standing up.

'Yeah, me too,' Frank agreed.

The rest rose and walked from the saloon together. Only Johnny O'Neal was left, his head drooped forward onto his chest, snoring softly.

9

'Three shells outa that one box misfired.'

Gar Newberry leaned across the counter at 'Eli's Furs And Firearms.' The owner of the establishment shrugged. 'That happens, Mr Newberry. I do not manufacture the ammunition, I merely sell it. But I certainly stand behind whatever I sell. Here are three cartridges to replace the ones that failed to work properly.'

Gar shook his head. 'That ain't good enough. I want a whole new box.'

Eli Lowenstein shook his own head in turn. 'That is not possible, Mr Newberry. I cannot give you an entire box of cartridges because of the misfire of three out of the fifty. I am willing to replace the faulty ones.'

'That ain't good enough,' Gar insisted more emphatically. 'That coulda cost me my life, or food for my table, or most anything. When I buy somethin', I expect it to work like it oughta.'

'Ah, it would indeed be a finer world if that were possible,' Eli commiserated. 'Unfortunately, any product made by man is subject to flaws and failures. Would that it were not so. But I am helpless to change that fact of life.'

'You don't hafta change that there fact o' life. You just have to gimme a new box o' shells.'

Eli shook his head again. 'As I said, I'm afraid I simply cannot do that. I should not stay in business very long if I were to go to that extreme in guaranteeing my merchandise.'

Several customers in Eli's store had stopped what they were doing and were watching the exchange with growing concern. Gar was growing increasingly agitated, and some of the customers were clearly concerned for the older storekeeper's well-being.

'You're gonna gimme a new box o' shells, and that's all there is to it!' Gar demanded.

Again Eli shook his head, speaking slowly, keeping his voice calm and reasonable. 'I will tell you what I will do, Mr Newberry, since you seem unduly upset by this matter. I will replace double the cartridges that you say misfired. That's more than generous, and that's the very best that I can do.'

'Whatd'ya mean, 'that I say misfired?'' Gar demanded, his voice rising a few more decibels. 'Are you sayin' they might not've misfired at all? Are you callin' me a liar?'

'I am doing nothing of the sort,' Eli objected. 'I'm merely observing that I'm willing to take your word at face value that three shells in that box misfired. I have offered to replace them doubly. That's more than generous, if I do say so.'

'I'll tell you what's more than generous,' Gar fumed. 'I'll let you keep your nose on the same side of your face it's on now if you give me the box of shells you owe me.'

It's never a prudent action to threaten a gunsmith's well-being when he's in his own environment. A slight movement of Eli's hand telegraphed his readiness to meet any violence with whatever was needed to defend himself. The action was not lost on Newberry.

Eli's face hardened. His words lost their conciliatory tone and took on a steely edge. 'Mr Newberry, I have tried to be more than fair with you. I do not take kindly to being threatened. Now I must ask that you leave my store. Here are six cartridges. You may take them or leave them, and I will hear no more of the matter. Go home and get your temper under control.'

Newberry's face turned from red to purple. He glanced around at the other customers. A couple of them returned his stare; others were suddenly very busy examining various items of merchandise. He glared back at Eli as he swept the half dozen forty-five cartridges from the counter and dropped them in his pocket. 'I'm leavin', but I'm tellin' you, Lowenstein, it's the last time you're kickin' me outa your store.'

He stormed out the door and stalked off up the street.

The store was silent for what seemed an inordinate amount of time, then everybody started talking at once.

'That Newberry is a problem. He's always mad at somebody.'

'He's a bully. Somebody's going to pull his horns in a notch or two one of these days.'

'That hand on the Circle T did a while back.'

'I heard he worked Newberry over pretty good.'

'Beat the livin' daylights out've him, and Newberry didn't lay a finger on 'im.'

'I'd be careful if I was you, Eli. He ain't a man to mess with.'

Eli shrugged. 'I am not easily intimidated,' he suggested. 'I am quite capable of defending myself, should it become necessary.'

'Yeah, I've seen that little shotgun

pistol you keep in your coat pocket,' a man concurred.

Eli smiled. 'There is that. There are other weapons readily available at hand should they be necessary. Now then, Henry, I believe you were next. How may I help you?'

With that the store returned to 'business as usual'.

It was a good day for Eli, discounting the confrontation with Newberry. He knew stories of that confrontation would have been carried all over town within an hour of its occurrence. That was just fine. All advertising is good for business.

As he counted up the day's receipts, Eli was pleased. He donned the light overcoat against the chill that descended quickly when the westering sun hovered close over the tops of the mountains. He stuffed the day's receipts into the left pocket of the coat, and, by habit, put his right hand in the other pocket where it found the familiar reassurance of the single-shot

410-gauge pistol. He had, himself, devised that pistol by placing a shotgun barrel on a single-shot .44 frame.

It was common knowledge that he carried that weapon. It was also common knowledge that he had at least one derringer and one larger pistol on his person at all times. He was, after all, a gunsmith. He was also a businessman. He often carried considerable amounts of money home from the store at night. He thought it a good deterrent to have it well known that he would not be an easy mark for anyone contemplating robbery.

He walked the length of the block, his shoes making only soft noises on the board sidewalk. At the corner he turned and started up the street toward his house. As he passed the back of the building that fronted onto the main street, a searing pain tore through his back, a little right of center.

The intensity of the pain took his breath away. It took a second for him to realize that he was under attack. Even as the large knife was jerked out of his back, he turned, pulling the pistol from the pocket of his coat. It was strangely heavy. His eyes darted here and there to find his attacker, and did not at once see him.

He heard, rather than saw, the presence of the other man. As he had turned, the man had moved so that he was still behind him. He spun as quickly as he could. He saw his attacker. His eyes widened in recognition. He tried to stop his turning and raise the gun. The gun was heavier still. The momentum of his turn seemed strangely difficult to stop. He continued to turn.

Something slammed against him, full length, driving the breath from his lungs. It took another second for him to realize it was the ground. He tried to lift himself from it, but his weight was suddenly more than he could lift. Darkness seemed to be rushing in upon him from all sides. He fought against it.

'No . . . ' he tried to say, but it came out as a mere whisper. The sound of the whisper sighed away into the enveloping darkness.

He never felt the hand that ripped the bag with the day's receipts from his coat pocket. Neither did he feel the small leather pouch that hung by a narrow leather strap from his neck being lifted over his head. He would no longer need the expensive watch that was removed from his pocket, or the short-barreled forty-five his killer's hand deftly slid from the leather-lined rear pocket the gunsmith thought nobody knew about. He never noticed that his attacker disappeared as silently as a shadow. His attention, by that time, was all enthralled by a world of peace and light, in which no murderous knives came out of nowhere to steal life away.

It was two hours later that his worried wife came upon his body as she walked toward the store in search of the husband who had not come home for supper. In spite of the lengthening shadows, she spotted him while she was scarcely out of her front gate. She ran to him, dropping to her knees. She screamed as she looked at her hand that had instinctively tried to turn the shopkeeper over. It was red with blood.

Her screams brought a crowd at once. People seemed to spill from the buildings and streets and lanes until a crowd was gathered around. Several people quickly checked the prone body and confirmed that Eli was, in fact, dead.

Conversation bubbled from everywhere in the crowd. Some expressed fright for their own safety. More expressed outrage. Many tried to speculate who might do such a thing.

A faceless voice in the crowd said, 'That no-account Potter guy was in town earlier today. I wouldn't put somethin' like this past him.'

'He ain't got the guts to do somethin' like this. Especially seein' as it ain't even plumb dark yet.'

'That half-breed that hangs around the livery barn would.'

'Yeah, but somebody'd know if he wasn't there when he's supposed to be workin'.'

Near the back of the crowd, the name Sam Murray was muttered softly by someone. The one who heard it asked the man next to him, 'What'd you say?'

'I didn't say nothin'.'

'I thought I heard somebody say the name 'Sam Murray'.'

'You mean that new guy at the Circle T?'

'That who it is? I don't know that I'd heard his name before.'

'What about him?'

'I don't know. I just heard somebody mention the name.'

A man standing close said, 'Somebody think he might have done it?'

'Not that I know of. I just heard someone say the name.'

'What name?'

'Sam Murray. From the Circle T.'

'Was he in town today?'

'I think he rode through earlier today anyway.'

'He didn't stay in town?'

'Might've. I don't know. What's Leah gonna do, you reckon?'

'No idea. Poor soul. Them with no kids, and now her husband gets killed like that. All alone in the world, she is.'

In a surprisingly short amount of time the storekeeper's body was removed to the undertaker's place. Leah was led back home by caring neighbors, who made plans for someone to stay with her for the night, and probably a few days beyond.

One of the neighbor ladies organized a plan for folks to bring food by the house for the next couple weeks, so Leah wouldn't have to worry about fixing her meals.

A group of the men retired to the Lucky Drover. There they hashed and rehashed all the possibilities they could think of, for who might be the culprit.

Once the name was mentioned there,

Gar Newberry seemed to make a point of bringing Sam's name up from time to time. He made no accusations. He just made note of the fact that he had noticed that Sam was in town today.

10

The three-quarter moon hung white and round in the afternoon sky. It would be dark in another hour or two, but the moon's light would be more than adequate to make the ride back to the Circle T easy.

It didn't matter. It could have been darker than the inside of a black cat in an unlighted cellar and Sam wouldn't have cared. In fact, it could have been thirty degrees below zero with a forty mile per hour wind in his face blowing snow in blinding flurries, and he wouldn't have cared. He might not have even noticed.

A few days before he had chanced to notice Frank, Greta, and Dorrie Birdwell in Big Springs at the same time he was there. Pouncing on the opportunity, he had immediately invited them to eat with him at the local café. If

116

Frank and Greta had felt any hesitancy, it wouldn't have mattered. Dorrie accepted the invitation so quickly and enthusiastically, they were left with no real options.

The owners of the Gadfly Ranch might just have been alone at the table anyway. Almost all the conversation was between Sam and Dorrie. They were so engrossed in each other that neither one even noticed when Frank and Greta finished eating. Frank winked at Greta, then got up quietly from the table. Glancing at the other two, Greta followed suit, careful not to scrape her chair legs on the floor. They walked to the counter, paid for all four meals, and left. It was some time before Sam and Dorrie even realized they were alone. Dinner time was long since over, and there were no other patrons left in the café.

Suddenly embarrassed at their preoccupation with each other, they got up hurriedly. Sam's embarrassment was heightened when he found out the rancher had already paid for the meals. He had invited them to that meal. It was an intolerable breach of etiquette, in his mind, that they had paid for it. Accordingly, he accompanied Dorrie to find them. When they caught up with them at the mercantile store, Frank instantly took advantage of the situation.

'Hey, Greta!' he called to his wife. 'Look who finally realized there wasn't anyone else at that table anymore.'

'Well, my, my!' Greta chimed in immediately. 'I was beginning to think you two were going to sit there staring into each other's eyes until it got too dark to see.'

'You weren't supposed to go payin' for dinner,' Sam asserted, ignoring the teasing jibes.

Frank shrugged. 'Well, the way you two was all lost in each other there, I was afraid they might start chargin' you interest on what you owed, so I thought I'd better go ahead and pay the bill.'

Dorrie rushed in to rescue Sam from

the teasing. 'I invited Sam out to supper day after tomorrow,' she said, facing her mother. 'Is that all right?'

Greta's eyebrows rose. It was clear from her expression that she thought Sam and Dorrie were rushing things much too fast, but she was at a loss for any way to object. 'Well, I, uh, sure! That'd be just fine.'

Day after tomorrow meant it was two days before Sam could see her again. He made up for the delay by arriving for supper shortly after noon on the appointed day. Dorrie suggested that, since they had a lot of time before supper, they should go for a ride, and she could show him some of the Gadfly Ranch.

They had, in fact, ridden for a ways. Then they had sat instead beside the creek that ran through that part of the ranch. Neither was nearly ready to respond when the supper bell pealed its summons over the hills.

After supper, as he prepared to mount his horse to leave, Dorrie abruptly stood on tiptoe and kissed him lightly on the lips, then whirled and disappeared into the house. Sam rode on a soft cloud of exhilaration all the way back to Big Springs.

He had intended to pass directly through town without stopping. After all, he'd been gone from the ranch where he was supposed to be working for most of the day. As chance would have it, Mort Halverson, his boss, was just coming out of the Lucky Drover as he rode past.

'Hey, Sam, you ridin' through without stoppin'?' he called.

'Uh, yeah. Yeah, I was just headin' back from Birdwell's. I, uh, I thought I oughta get back to the place,' Sam replied, feeling like a kid that had been caught at the fishing hole when he was supposed to be in school.

'Just as well. Folks ain't in a very friendly mood in town today.'

'Why? What happened?'

'Somebody killed Eli Lowenstein.'

'The gunsmith?'

'Yup. Waylaid 'im on his way home. Stabbed 'im in the back, right here in the middle o' town, and not even after dark or nothin'.'

'You don't say! Someone with a grudge against 'im?'

'Don't think so. Could be, I guess. It looks more like just plain robbery. Needless to say, folks are pretty riled up about it.'

'I can imagine. Well, that explains all the activity. I thought there was a lot of people out and about tonight.'

'I don't know what the country's comin' to,' the rancher lamented. 'A man can't even close up his business and walk home in broad daylight and be safe anymore.'

'Any idea who did it?'

'Oh, sure, everybody's got an idea or two. Everybody that's been seen in town durin' the past week has been mentioned at least once or twice. Not to mention a few folks that ain't been within fifty miles o' here. The only one I ain't heard mentioned is the Pope. I figger he's in the clear. Nobody knows, though.'

'Well, I don't guess I'd have anything to add to all the conversation about it. I still think I'll just head on out to the place. You didn't get much work out've me today.'

Mort chuckled. 'Aw, you pull your weight for dang sure. Besides, we'll make up for today, sooner or later. Not to mention that the boys can all most likely get tucked into bed by theirselves. But since you're so all-fired anxious to make up for wastin' most o' this day, I'll tell what I do need for you to do. There's a bunch o' steers in that long valley that runs east from Chalk Bluff. Do you know the valley I'm talkin' about?'

Sam nodded his head. 'I've never been there, but I know where it is.'

'Well, at the head of that valley, there's a nice spring that forms the beginnin' o' Clear Crick. Ed an' a couple o' the boys'll be headin' up there come mornin'. Instead o' you ridin' clear back out to the place an' then turnin' right around an' ridin' back tomorrow, why don't you just ride on up there tonight. It ain't more'n a couple hours' ride from town here. You can camp there by the spring, so the other boys'll know where to find you. Then first thing in the mornin' you can locate them steers, an' maybe get 'em started bunchin' together. Then the four of you can move 'em up onto some o' the high grass to fatten.'

Sam glanced up at the sky. The moon would be well up before the sun set. There'd be plenty of light to ride by to get where he needed to go and pitch camp. It would make a short night's sleep, but better than if he had to ride clear out to the ranch tonight and then back in the morning. 'Sounds like a lot less ridin' to me,' he agreed. 'Not that I mind, you understand, but my horse could use the break.'

'Yeah, I'm sure you been workin' that horse real hard while you been wranglin' steers up at the Gadfly place.'

Sam swallowed the jibe without comment. The rancher walked to his own horse and mounted. He looked at his newest hired hand a long moment, then said, 'For whatever it's worth, you could do a whole lot worse. That Birdwell gal is as fine a woman as you're gonna find. The Birdwells are old friends o' mine, though. I'd not take it kindly if you was to take advantage of her, or hurt her in any way.'

'I sure don't intend to do that,' Sam promised.

Mort nodded, turned his horse and headed out of town toward the Circle T. Sam turned his own mount and headed out of town in the other direction.

Two sets of ears, one that remained totally unseen and one that pretended not to be listening, digested the information. Both abruptly changed their plans for the rest of the night.

11

'It had to be somebody that knowed Eli's routine.'

'Not necessarily. Somebody coulda just seen 'im closin' up, and followed him.'

The first speaker shook his head. 'Nah, I don't think so. Old Eli was pretty cagey. He kept his hand on that shotgun pistol he always had in his coat pocket, and kept his eyes open. If anyone was followin' 'im, he'da spotted 'em.'

'So you think it was someone that knowed where Eli lived, and just waited outa sight for 'im to come by on his way home?'

'Makes the most sense to me. That's why he could shove a knife in his back before he had a chance to even call out.'

'So it had to be somebody that

knowed him and knowed where he lived.'

'Someone we all know, sure's anything.'

'If we talk it through, I'm bettin' we can figger out who it most likely was.'

'There ain't that many people in Big Springs that'd do such a thing.'

Felix Walker stirred himself from his near stupor long enough to mutter in his slurred speech, 'I did see that new fella in town earlier. He was more interested in needlin' Gar than anythin' else, though.'

Nobody appeared to notice the comment. Felix slouched back down into his chair, his chin dropping to his chest. As he did, he slurred drunkenly, 'Newberry's the only one I know that's always had a chip on his shoulder for Eli, though.'

Newberry pushed himself erect at the back end of the bar. 'Who said that? Who'd I hear shovin' my name into this?'

Nobody offered to claim the comment. Felix rose from the chair in which he was slouched. He held on to the table for a while, fighting for balance. Then he walked with steps far too deliberate and careful to the front door and outside. He started to stagger sideways once, but quickly caught himself without having to grab onto anything for support, and continued on his way. Ignoring him, Gar glared around at the scattered patrons of the saloon, his look daring anybody to make the accusation to his face.

Finally, from a table of cowboys, one said, 'Now that it's been brought up it seems like you was the one that knew right where that necklace was in Eff's saddle-bag, though, Newberry. How'd you happen to look right where it was?'

Gar's face turned deep red as his eyes flashed with instant wrath. 'You sayin' I planted that thing in his saddle-bag?' he challenged.

The cowboy, backed by three of his friends, buoyed by more than a couple drinks, was in no mood to back down. 'The thought did cross my mind.'

Unused to being challenged directly, Gar blinked several times. Finally he said, 'Well I can tell you for danged sure it wasn't me. But whoever said it is right. I did see that Sam Murray in town twice today. I seen 'im in town this mornin'; I seen 'im again not more'n an hour ago.'

When nobody responded, Gar pressed the issue, blatantly trying to divert suspicion from himself. 'As a matter o' fact, I heard him and Mort talkin', and he's gonna be camped up at Clear Crick spring tonight. It'd sure be easy to ride up there and check him out. You all know I been in here all evenin'. If Murray's got Eli's stuff, you'll know there ain't no way I coulda put it there.'

A buzz of conversation seemed to wend its way around the saloon like a swarm of bees that couldn't decide where to land. More than an hour later, the cowboy that had directly challenged Newberry finally said, 'If we ride up there and check 'im out, and if we find somethin' of Eli's in his stuff, we're bringin' 'im back to town. There ain't gonna be another lynchin' that we find out later was the wrong guy.'

A mutter of agreement swept around the room. As it died away, everybody simply stayed where they were. Clearly they all wanted to go find out if Sam had anything to do with the robbery, but nobody wanted to be the one to instigate it.

Almost predictably it was Newberry who became the necessary catalyst. 'Well if we're gonna do it, let's do it. We can get up there while the moon's still up.'

He slammed his beer mug on the bar and headed for the door. By the time he went out the front door half a dozen men had risen to join him.

12

Sam found the spring with no trouble at all. As he approached, several deer bounded into the surrounding timber.

'Nice to know nobody else is around,' Sam commented to his horse. 'Them deer would've sensed 'em for sure if they were.'

He unsaddled his horse and hobbled him. He removed the bridle, and the animal immediately began munching on the lush grass.

Finding a tree with a horizontal branch about the right height, he threw his lariat over the limb, hooked the loop around the saddle-horn, then hoisted the saddle high enough to keep the skunks, racoons, chipmunks, or other nocturnal critters from gnawing on the leather. Drawn by the salt of countless sweaty days, he knew the leather would be irresistible to them otherwise.

He spread out his blankets. He took a tin cup and walked to the spring. Dipping it into the icy water by the soft moonlight, he lifted it to his lips and drank long and with relish. Finished, he whipped the cup as if to fling out any remaining moisture and wiped the back of a hand across his mouth. 'Good water,' he muttered.

He removed his boots, slid his forty-five beneath the rolled up blanket he used for a pillow, pulled the rest of the blankets over himself, and was asleep in minutes.

He had been asleep for nearly three hours when a shadow separated itself from the edge of the timber. The shadow stayed motionless for a long moment. Then it glided silently forward. Beneath the large hat, a pair of eyes roamed constantly around, never looking directly at Sam. Whoever it was seemed well aware that even a sleeping man may feel another pair of eyes looking at him. He placed his feet carefully, not making the least noise as he crept forward. He paused at Sam's suspended saddle. Glancing once at the sleeping cowboy, he lifted the flap of a saddle-bag and thrust something inside. Closing the flap on the saddle-bag again, he turned and melted into the timber as silently as he had appeared. The shadow of a hawk in the moonlight slid across the campsite. It made no more noise than the shadow that had preceded it.

Sam stirred in his blankets, wriggled himself into a more comfortable spot between humps in the ground, and went back to sleep.

Minutes later another shadow moved across the open space. It moved just as deliberately to Sam's saddle. Smaller than the previous shadow, it stretched upward. A hand fished around in Sam's saddle-bag. After a moment it emerged clutching something. Instantly the shadow headed for the timber.

Just as the shadow merged into the darkness of the trees, a small twig snapped beneath a foot. Sam sprang from his bed, rolled sideways into a crouch, his forty-five pointed unerringly at the spot from which the noise had come. 'Who's there?' he demanded.

Even as he spoke, he moved sideways into the cover of the trees. He caught a fleeting movement ahead where a gap in the trees allowed a little moonlight to penetrate. Holding his fire, he called, 'Hold it right there!'

Whoever it was failed to obey. There was no more movement. There was no more sound. As silently as he could, walking carefully to avoid anything that would hurt his stockinged feet, he crept toward where he had last seen that hint of movement. He made a wide circle and came back to his campsite. He found nothing. He heard nothing. He sensed nothing more. Whatever was there was gone. 'Must've just been a varmint of some sort,' he shrugged.

He slid back into his blankets. It took him a little longer to get back to sleep, but before long he was, once again, sleeping deeply.

Even so, he heard them before they arrived. Maybe a horse's hoof had struck a rock. Maybe his own horse had huffed a greeting to another horse. Maybe a saddle had creaked. Whatever it was that woke him, he was instantly awake and alert.

Once again he slid from his blankets and into the protective darkness of the timber, pistol in hand. He crouched there against the trunk of a pine tree for several minutes. Then he heard them again. He mentally counted at least half a dozen horses. He almost chuckled as he heard them admonishing one another to be quiet. If they hadn't already wakened him, their efforts to keep each other quiet certainly would have.

'Sounds like they spent way too much time drinkin' and plannin',' he muttered to himself.

He clearly heard them dismount twenty or thirty feet away from where his blankets were spread. He heard their whispered consultations as they spread out into a line and started forward, clearly seeking him. When seven of them had stepped into the clearing, Sam said, 'You boys lookin' for somethin'?'

As he spoke he silently moved sideways, just in case somebody decided to shoot at the sound of his voice. Three of the men carried rifles. The others had pistols, but they were all still in their holsters.

'Are you Sam Murray?' the unmistakable voice of Gar Newberry demanded.

'That's me, Newberry. You bring along some help this time, did you?'

He could feel, rather than see, the rising anger in the big man. Instead of answering, Newberry said, 'Why don't you quit hidin' in the timber an' step out here like a man?'

'Well, the biggest reason is that I don't want to have to shoot any of you boys. Why are you tryin' to sneak up on my camp, and what do you want?'

'We wanta know where you been all day.'

135

'And just why would that be any of your business?'

A different voice spoke up. 'Somebody killed Eli Lowenstein today. We wanta know, was you in town when it happened?'

'Nope. As a matter of fact I wasn't. I was in town later. Mort told me about it when I was ridin' through, and he sent me back up here. But from what Mort told me, I'd've still been out at the Gadfly place when it happened.'

'You got any witnesses to that?'

'Well, yeah, if I need 'em. The whole Birdwell family will vouch for when I left there.'

'You got some business with them?'

'Now that's somethin' that's not any of your business at all.'

Newberry spoke up again. 'In that case, I'm sure you wouldn't mind if we was to take a look in your saddle-bags, now would you?'

Alarm bells sounded in Sam's mind. He thought back over all the time he had been in town. He hadn't even gotten off his horse while he talked to Mort. There was no way anybody could possibly have put anything in his saddle-bags.

Then he remembered something had wakened him earlier. He remembered the talk of the planted evidence that had condemned Ephraim Harris to an untimely death. He was instantly certain the noise he had heard in his sleep was somebody putting something in his saddle-bags. That somebody, in his mind, almost certainly wore the name of Gar Newberry. Even knowing what was going on, he couldn't think of any way to prevent them from looking in those saddle-bags.

'Knock yourselves out,' he said, sounding as nonchalant as he could manage.

Instantly, Gar strode to Sam's saddle. He whipped open the flap on a saddle-bag and reached inside. His hand fished around for a while, and emerged empty. He turned the saddle so the other side was next to him and examined the other compartment. He lifted out several items, one at a time, but clearly nothing that he was looking for.

Obviously frustrated, he turned to the others. 'There's nothin' in there. Look around his camp. Look in his blankets. Check them boots sittin' there.'

Sam watched with growing anger while they rifled through his things. Finally they looked at each other, clearly feeling more and more like they had been manipulated and embarrassed. One of them, the same cowboy that had challenged Newberry in the saloon, finally said, 'Well, Newberry, you satisfied? You talked us all into makin' fools of ourselves for nothin'. I'm goin' back to town.'

Without a word the others turned and walked toward their horses. Before they were out of sight, one of them turned back. 'Hey, Sam. I'm sorry about this here.'

'Who talked you into bein' another

lynch mob?' Sam demanded.

'It wasn't gonna be no lynch mob,' another insisted. 'We agreed afore we started out that even if we found anything o' Eli's in your stuff, that we was bringin' you back to town an' that's all.'

Unconvinced, Sam retorted, his voice heavy with sarcasm, 'Yeah, that's why you brought the marshal with you, huh?'

The absence of any law enforcement officer with them screamed more loudly than any of their denials possibly could. The others all looked back and forth at each other as if trying to figure out which of them seemed to be the most idiotic. Finally one who hadn't spoken up yet addressed Gar. 'This was mostly your idea, as I recall, Newberry. Exactly what was it you had planned? You weren't by chance plannin' on usin' us to get even with Sam for that whuppin' he put on you, was you?'

Angry comments began to fly as it quickly became a contest to see who was the most offended by the actions they now unanimously assigned to Newberry. Mob psychology is a strange and unpredictable thing. For a couple minutes it appeared as if Gar himself might end up being the victim of an impromptu lynching.

It was Sam who brought a voice of reason back to the escalating anger of the group. 'It ain't gonna do any good for you boys to shift the blame onto Newberry. You rode up here on your own. Now you'd best ride back to town on your own as well, before somebody ends up gettin' hurt.'

There was a long moment of silence. Then, almost as one, the group turned and headed once again for their horses. As they passed out of hearing, the last comment Sam heard was, 'It's gonna be a mighty cold day in July when I ever listen to another thing you say, Newberry.'

When they had gone, Sam stayed where he was for a long moment. Silence returned to the mountainside.

The moon hovered low in the west, casting the land in deeper shadow. Still Sam stayed where he was, waiting, listening.

Nearly an hour had passed when he caught the slightest whisper of sound off to his left. He stiffened, straining his eyes and ears. Minutes later a shadow separated itself from the deeper shadow of a clump of brush and crept toward his campsite. A dozen feet from his blankets, it stopped. The shadow hovered there, seeming to be confused. Then a soft voice said, 'Mister?'

The sound of the voice startled Sam more than anything that had happened in an already strange night. It was the voice of a child! 'Who are you?' he answered, keeping his voice just as soft.

The shadow jumped when Sam's voice came from an unexpected direction. Sam thought he was going to run, but instead he said, 'Tad.'

'Tad who?'

'Newberry.'

Sam felt the blood drain from his

face. 'Are you Gar's boy?'

'Yessir.'

'What are you doin' out here? Are you on foot? Do you have a horse? Does your pa know you're here?'

As is often the case with a lot of folks, Sam couldn't restrain himself from asking a whole string of questions before he got an answer to any of them. Therefore he had no idea which of his questions Tad was answering when he said in a voice that sounded as if even the syllables sought to hide beneath the nearest bush, 'No.'

The shadow of his presence disappeared. Sam called out, louder than he intended, 'Now don't go skedaddlin' on me! Where'd you go?'

From a spot a little ways distant, the boy's voice said, 'Over here.'

Forcing himself to ask one question at a time, Sam said, 'Are you on foot?'

'Yessir.'

'You came all the way out here from town on foot?'

'Yessir.'

'Why?'

There was a long hesitance. 'I didn't want my pa gettin' in any more trouble.'

'Why would your pa be in trouble?'

'People think he killed the Jew.'

'Did he?'

'No, sir.'

'Are you sure?'

'Yessir.'

'But if you weren't here, people would think he did?'

'Yessir.'

'Why?'

There was another long silence. Finally a shadow separated itself from the deeper shadows of the timber. The boy walked purposefully up to Sam. He held out a hand. Something dangled from his fingers. Sam reached out and took a small leather pouch that had a leather thong attached to each end.

'What's this?'

'It was the Jew's.'

'This belonged to Eli?'

'Yessir.'

'How did you get it?'

'I took it out of your saddle-bag. Before they all got here.'

Sam's mind swam with confusion. It was a full minute before he asked, 'You took it from my saddle-bag? How did it get there?'

'The one that killed the . . . that killed Mr Lowenstein put it there.'

'Do you know what it is?'

'He . . . Mr Lowenstein . . . he always wore it around his neck. He told me about it once. It has a name.'

'A name? This thing has a name?'

'Yessir.'

'What's its name?'

'Phil.'

'Phil?'

'Yessir. Well, I guess that's just its first name.'

'It has a last name too?'

'Yessir, but it's hard to say.'

'What does it sound like?'

'Acktry, or something like that.'

'Phil Acktry,' Sam repeated. Then he said it again, fast enough it sounded as

144

if it were all one name. 'Phil Acktry.'

'He always wore it,' the boy repeated.

The word made no sense to Sam, but he asked, 'So why would somebody put it in my saddle-bag?'

'To make people think you killed him. But he knew it wouldn't work.'

Sam felt his blood turn to ice as the implications of the boy's words sunk in. Then the rest of what the boy said registered. 'Why wouldn't it work?'

'Cuz it was just like before. Only afterwards everyone found out that necklace was just put there by someone. So when he did it again, they'd think this was put there by the same someone to try to get you hunged like he did that other guy.'

It was the most words at one time he had ever heard the boy speak, and he wasn't following his logic at all. Instead of pursuing it immediately, he said, 'And you come all the way out here on foot to keep it from happening?'

'Yessir.'

'Why did you know to come here?'

'I followed him.'

'Followed who?'

The barest hesitation was followed by the hurried statement, 'I gotta go now.'

The shadow that indicated the boy's presence melted into the timber and disappeared. Sam strained to hear something to indicate where he had gone. There was no sound. After a minute or two he said, 'Tad?'

There was no answer.

'Tad? I need for you to tell me who it is.'

His voice bounced back from the darkness. The boy was gone as silently as the shadow of the hawk that had passed overhead.

'Now if that don't beat all,' he muttered, staring in the darkness at 'Phil Acktry' in his hand. 'I wonder what this thing really is. And I wonder why he's trying so hard to keep his pa out of trouble, especially considerin' the way his pa treats 'im. For that matter, I wonder if he's even tellin' me the truth that his pa didn't kill Eli.'

The darkness offered no answers to any of his questions.

13

There was no sleep for Sam the rest of the night. Even knowing he wasn't going to be successful, he moved his blankets into the timber a ways where he felt more secure, and tried to sleep. He may have dozed off a time or two, but he wasn't sure he'd slept at all after the self-appointed posse had left.

He finally gave up on the idea of sleep. He built a small fire, made coffee, and fixed himself some breakfast. Well before daylight he was in the saddle. He found the steers easily and had them bunched and already moving toward the high country when the others from the Circle T found him.

'You been workin' all night?' Ed demanded.

'I'd be less tired if I had been,' Sam grumbled.

He had the attention of all three of

the Circle T riders instantly. He filled them in on the events of the night before, but left out all mention of the boy, or of the item that had been planted in his saddle-bag.

'Newberry,' was the instant response from Cap Baker.

'Maybe,' Sam agreed. 'I ain't sure, though.'

'Well, who else would it be?' Cap demanded.

He almost said, 'Maybe it's just someone trying to frame Newberry for trying to frame me,' but even before he said it, it sounded completely inane even to himself.

'Now that I couldn't say,' Sam admitted, instead of what he wanted to say. 'It just seems too obvious.'

'Well, we ain't gonna solve none of it by sittin' here chinnin',' Ed, the straw boss, growled. 'Let's get these critters moved.'

Because of the head start Sam's sleepless night had provided, they had the steers relocated by noon and headed back to the Circle T. As they passed within a hundred yards of a neck of timber, a movement within the trees caught Sam's eye. His head jerked in that direction, even as his hand dropped to his gun butt. For the barest instant he clearly saw Tad Newberry step out from behind a tree, then duck back again. He was certain the boy's purpose was to be seen by him.

He reined in his horse. So also did Cap Baker, whose sharp eyes seldom missed anything. 'Was that there meant to catch your eye?' he demanded.

Sam frowned. 'I'm guessin' so.'

'Who's the kid?'

Sam hesitated a short moment, then said, 'Tad Newberry.'

'Gar's kid?'

Ed and Lennie Lewis, the other hand that had participated in the day's work, noticed the other two had stopped. They turned and rode back. 'Somethin' wrong?' Ed inquired.

Watching the timber carefully, Sam said, 'I ain't sure.'

'Would the kid sucker you into a trap?' Cap suggested.

The thought had already occurred to Sam. 'I don't think so, but I ain't sure.'

'Why would he be wantin' to talk to you?'

Again Sam hesitated as three sets of eyes drilled holes in him. He took a deep breath. He rode with these men. They all rode for the brand. If he couldn't trust them, he'd just as well ride out of the country now. Briefly he filled them in on the part of last night he had kept to himself.

'You think the kid's tellin' the truth?' Ed demanded.

Sam shrugged. 'Maybe. Or maybe his pa's tellin' 'im what to do and say, and he's scared to do anything different. He's taken some awful whippin's.'

'Everybody knows that, for sure,' Lennie agreed.

'So what're you gonna do?' Cap demanded.

'Well, I guess I'll ride over there and see what he wants.'

'And get your dang fool head blowed off.'

Sam frowned again. 'If his pa has 'im tryin' to draw me into a trap, he'd just as well have shot me off my horse already. We're sure in easy range of anyone in the timber already, while we're sittin' here jawin'.'

'That's what's makin' the hair crawl on the back o' my neck,' Cap agreed.

'If we spread out and ride into the timber we can come toward where he's at from all sides,' Ed suggested.

Sam shook his head. 'I've seen that kid in the timber. When he wants to, he just plumb disappears like a shadow when the sun ducks behind a cloud. One second he's standin' right there, and the next he's just gone. And he does it without makin' a sound. We'd never see 'im if we tried to corral 'im.'

'He must be able to cover a lot o' country on foot, too,' Lennie observed, 'If he beat that bunch from town out to where you was camped.'

'Which means he's probably long

gone already,' Cap offered, almost hopefully.

'Not likely,' Sam disagreed. 'He must wanta talk to me. Why don't you boys ride on a couple hundred yards or so and wait. I'll ride up to the timber and see what he wants.'

The three stared at him as if he'd just offered to go grab a mountain lion by the tail to see if he'd squeal. Cap shrugged and said, 'It's your funeral. Any place special you want buried?'

'Yeah. Right out in back of the old folks' home where I've died of old age,' Sam said as he reined his horse toward the timber.

He rode slowly to allow the others to get far enough away to, he hoped, make Tad comfortable enough to show himself. At the edge of the timber he pulled his horse to a stop and said, 'Where you at, Tad?'

Almost instantly Tad was standing twenty feet from him, as if he had been there all along. Sam jumped in spite of himself.

'I'm sorta hungry,' Tad said.

Sam considered the statement, then reached back into a saddle-bag. 'I ain't got much with me but a hunk o' jerky and a couple o' biscuits that're harder'n rocks.'

The boy's eyes lit up. 'I can chew 'em.'

Sam handed them to the lad and he started chewing on the jerky with obvious urgency.

'You been back home since last night?' Sam asked.

Tad stopped chewing just long enough to say, 'Yessir. I hadta leave pretty quick, though.'

'Why?'

'Cuz he spotted me comin' back into town. I think he figgered out I know what he's doin'.'

'He tried to do somethin' to you?'

'He tried to catch me.'

'That'd be kinda like tryin' to catch the wind,' Sam observed.

Tad ignored the comment, busily chewing on the jerky. With surprising ease he chewed off a corner from one of the biscuits and began rolling it around in his mouth to soften it.

'He's eaten a few dried-out biscuits before,' crossed Sam's mind.

Aloud he said, 'Who is it?'

Tad's eyes widened and focused on Sam's for the barest instant. In that instant Sam saw a fear that was stark and deep. The boy looked away instantly. He shook his head wordlessly, concentrating on the biscuit and jerky.

Sam lifted his canteen and held it out to the boy. 'Here. You better wet your whistle or that stuff will suck the moisture out've you like a spider does to a fly.'

The lad took the canteen, drank greedily, then put the lid back on and passed it back. He stopped eating for a moment and looked at Sam, clearly trying to make a decision. 'I can't go back to town.'

'Why not?'

'He'll be watchin' for me. I seen what he does to somethin' that crosses 'im.'

'Like what?'

Tad looked all around as if worrying about somebody eavesdropping. Then he said, 'He got bit by a dog once. When nobody was lookin', he grabbed the dog by the scruff o' the neck an' hauled 'im off to that gully north o' town. Nobody could hear the dog a-yelpin' an' howlin' from there. He done real bad things. He hurt that dog plumb awful afore he went an' kilt 'im. He's crazy mean.'

At a loss for words, Sam watched the boy eat for several minutes. Finally he said, 'So what are you going to do if you can't go back to town?'

The fear flashed in the boy's eyes again briefly, then he shrugged his thin shoulders.

'You can't just stay hid out in the timber.'

He shrugged again.

Sam took a deep breath, thinking feverishly. Finally an idea dawned. 'If I take you to some folks that I trust,

156

someplace he won't even think about lookin' for you, will you stay there?'

Tad looked fully at him for the first time, studying his face carefully. 'Where?'

'The Gadfly.'

'Birdwell's place?'

'Yeah.'

The boy was thoughtful again. 'They'll know where I am,' he said, nodding his head toward the trio of Circle T hands waiting three hundred yards away.

'Yeah. But they'll keep their mouths shut.'

'Will they let me sleep in the hay mow?'

'Why? They'll have a bed in the house for you.'

He shook his head. 'In the hay mow I can hear someone comin'. The animals always know. If he finds out I'm there, I got a chance to get away if I'm in the barn.'

Sam thought it over. He couldn't argue with the boy's logic. He knew he'd do the same if their roles were reversed. 'They will if I ask them to,' he promised.

'You sweet on Dorrie?'

The question caught Sam completely by surprise. Was there anything that went on in town the boy didn't know? 'Why?' was the only thing he could think of to say.

'She's nice,' was Tad's only answer. 'She'll do what you ask?'

'She'll do what I ask.'

His decision clearly made, Tad said, 'Okay.' Then he pointed to the other three riders. 'Do they have to know?'

'Yeah. I work for the Circle T. They have to know where I'm going and why.'

He thought it over a moment, then shrugged. Sam said, 'Climb up behind me.'

He kicked a foot out of the stirrup to give the lad a foothold. He didn't need it. He grabbed the cantle of Sam's saddle and leaped like a deer, landing atop Sam's bedroll. Sam reined his horse around and rode to where the

158

others waited. He filled them in on what he knew as Tad finished consuming the jerky and biscuits.

Cap rode up beside them and handed the boy a packet with half a dozen thick slices of cooked bacon and a lard sandwich. 'Here,' he said, his voice as gruff as he could pretend. 'You better chew on these awhile. I don't want ya eatin' the cantle offa Sam's saddle afore you get there.'

14

It was four hours later that the pair rode into the yard of the G Bar F ranch.

'Oh, Sam! You look terrible! Are you all right?'

Sam stepped from the saddle, surprised and thrilled as Dorrie flung herself into his arms. He held her close, all sense of fatigue washing out of his body, replaced by the heady sense of her presence.

She stepped back away from him, suddenly embarrassed by her lack of decorum. 'I'm sorry,' she blushed. 'That was terribly forward of me.'

Self-consciousness rendered his responding grin slightly askew. 'You didn't hear any complaint outa me, did you?'

Instead of answering she said, 'Who's your friend?'

Extending a hand toward the boy

who still sat atop his bedroll, Sam said, 'Dorrie, this here's Tad Newberry. Tad, this is Dorrie.'

'I seen you in town some,' Tad responded. His voice was quiet enough to sound timid.

Dorrie's eyes darted back and forth between Sam and Tad. They asked a dozen silent questions that, for a moment, Sam was too lost in the green depths of her eyes to notice. He might have just stood there staring stupidly into those limpid pools for hours if Frank and Greta Birdwell hadn't stepped out onto the porch.

'I thought we'd got rid of you for a few days,' was Frank's dry greeting.

Greta elbowed him in the ribs. 'Frank! That's not nice!'

To Sam she said, 'We didn't expect you back quite so soon. Is something wrong?'

Sam took a deep breath. He looked at Greta, then at Frank, then his eyes were drawn back to Dorrie's. 'It's kind've a long story,' he said.

161

'Well then, for goodness' sake,' Greta huffed, 'come on inside and share it with us. I was just getting ready to set supper on the table, and Frank was scolding me for cooking so much. Now I know why I did.'

Tad slid off the horse and started toward the steps. Then he abruptly stopped and looked back at Sam, as if afraid he'd just about done something wrong.

Greta picked up on his hesitancy at once. 'Don't wait for those two,' she said, nodding a head toward Sam and Dorrie. 'We may be half done with supper before they make it across the porch.'

As she spoke she held a hand out toward Tad in open invitation. As he passed through the door Greta said, 'There's a wash pan and towel just inside the kitchen door. By the time you get washed up, I'll have it on the table.'

Frank turned and followed his wife and Tad into the house. Dorrie stood looking up into Sam's eyes. 'Something's wrong, isn't it?'

'It's gonna be all right,' he offered, even though the words sounded to him as lame as they must have sounded to her.

'What is it?'

He thought it over a long moment, then said, 'Why don't we go on in. I can explain it to all three of you at the same time.'

'Well, one reason is because we're alone here right now.'

Sam took off his hat and made a show of smoothing his hair while he looked around the ranch yard. She was right. There was nobody in sight at all.

As he turned back toward her, he found her almost against him, her head tilted back, her lips slightly parted. It was an invitation he wasted no time in accepting.

'I've missed you terribly already,' she asserted as their lips parted.

'I wasn't sure I was even gonna get to

see you again for a little bit there,' he confessed.

Her eyes instantly reflected the fear engendered by his words. 'What on earth happened?' she asked once again.

Instead of answering, he said, 'Let's go eat.'

Irritation flashed briefly in her eyes, replaced by reluctant acquiescence. The feel of his arm around her waist made it impossible for her to be angry.

Sam washed quickly, flung the wash basin of water out the back door of the kitchen, replaced the basin on its stand, and sat down in the only empty chair at the table. It didn't immediately occur to him that it just chanced to be next to Dorrie.

The five of them ate in silence until their plates were cleaned. Tad glanced at the bowls of food that were only half empty on the table, then back at his plate. He lowered his eyes.

'Would you like seconds?' Greta asked immediately. 'We're going to have an awful lot of food left over here if you don't help us eat it up.'

As they watched the slight waif of a lad devour a second, then a third plateful of the food, Sam told them about the visit from the posse.

The three maintained silence as long as they could, then questions sprouted like weeds after a spring rain.

'Eli Lownstein was killed?'

'Someone thought you killed him?'

'A posse knew where to find you?'

'Someone put something in your saddle-bag?'

'Someone in the posse knew it was there?'

'What was it?'

'How did you convince them you didn't put it there?'

Sam answered only the last question. 'Tad slipped in behind the guy that put it there, and took it out again, so when they looked for it, it wasn't there.'

'What was it?'

Sam reached into his pocket and withdrew the leather pouch with its thongs that had held it around the merchant's neck. Their eyes widened. 'It's Eli's phylactery!' Dorrie exclaimed.

'Tad said Eli named it Phil something.'

'Phylactery,' Dorrie repeated.

It was Sam's turn to ask, 'What is it?'

Frank explained, 'It's one o' them things some Jews wear all the time. It's got a piece o' paper inside of it.'

'Yeah, I found that. It looks like some kind of writing on it, but I can't read what it says,' Sam confirmed.

'It's Hebrew,' Frank said. 'It's that Bible verse that says, 'Hear O Israel, the Lord our God, the Lord is One. Thou shalt love the Lord thy God with all thy heart and with all thy soul and with all thy strength.' I asked him about it once. I sorta thought he'd be put off some by me askin', but he wasn't. He told me all about it, like he was kinda proud of it.'

Greta suddenly made the connection with Eli's murder. The sharp intake of her breath drew every eye at the table to her, except for Tad's. He was still devoting his whole attention to the rapidly diminishing food on his plate.

'Whoever took it had to be the one that killed him!'

'Yup. Looks that way.'

'And it was put in your saddle-bag to make it look like you're the one that did it.'

'Yup. Looks that way.'

'Newberry! He's still tryin' to get even with you for the whippin' you laid on 'im.'

Tad stopped shoveling in the food long enough to look around and wait for someone to answer the accusation. It was Sam who did so. 'Tad says not. He knows who it was, but he ain't sayin'.'

'Why not, Tad?' Dorrie demanded. 'Why won't you tell us who it is?'

The boy stopped eating long enough to say, 'Cuz he'd kill me.'

Silence clamped the circumference of the table as tightly as Tad's lid on the coveted information. He ignored it, returning to his food.

Finally Dorrie asked, 'Well who

would it have been, if it wasn't Newberry?'

'Tad says it's the same guy that put the necklace in that cowboy's saddle-bag.'

'Eff Harris.'

'Yeah. That's the guy. But when Eli was killed, and the posse found that phil . . . whatever — '

'Phylactery,' Dorrie supplied.

'Yeah. That thing. When they found it in my saddle-bag, Tad figures they'd know I was bein' set up, just like Harris was. Then they'd blame his dad.'

Silence returned as each struggled with the idea. Clearly nobody thought it sounded very reasonable. It was Dorrie that asked, 'Tad, does anyone else know who the killer really is?'

Tad looked at her for longer than Sam could remember him returning anyone's stare. He looked down again. His voice was soft. 'Maybe Moose. I dunno.'

'Moose?' Sam echoed.

'Harold Lutz,' Frank explained. 'The

hostler at the livery barn.'

'Oh.'

'Folks call him, 'Moose', 'cause he's big and not too bright.'

'He's not nearly as dumb as people think,' Dorrie defended.

'His wife is Doc Stringwell's nurse and secretary,' Frank inserted.

'And I don't for the life of me understand what that beautiful young lady sees in that big, slow-witted ape of a man,' Greta fussed. 'She is a brilliant person; almost as able to treat most things as Dr Stringwell himself.'

'Moose ain't as dumb as folks think he is,' Frank echoed Dorrie's words. 'He's the best hand with horses I've ever seen in my life. There ain't a horse comes in that livery barn with anything wrong with it that he don't spot. Nine times out of ten he knows exactly what to do about it, too. He's got salves and liniments and concoctions that'll fix 'most anything from saddle sores to spavin to who knows what.'

'I still think Esther could have done a

lot better. She could have had her pick of men in the whole area.'

'She did,' Frank reminded her, 'and she chose Moose.'

Greta opened her mouth and closed it again twice. Sam couldn't help but notice Dorrie's glee at her mother's discomfiture. She was grinning openly, her eyes dancing, watching to see how her mother would respond. Finally Greta acknowledged, 'They do seem to be terribly happy together.'

'There ain't much goes on in town that Moose don't notice, neither,' Frank opined. 'Prob'ly 'cause folks think he's too dumb to matter, they don't worry about him much. The boy just might be right. He might have a pretty good idea who the killer is.'

After a bit, Sam cleared his throat. 'Uh, Tad says the guy that really did it most likely knows he's the one that messed up the plan. He's convinced if he goes back to town, the guy'll kill him. I was wonderin' if maybe he could stay here with you folks, till we get things sorted out.'

'Oh, of course!' Greta said, without hesitation. 'We have two extra bedrooms.'

Sam looked uncomfortable. 'Uh, the thing is, he don't wanta stay here in the house.'

'What?'

'He's afraid the guy'll come here lookin' for 'im. If he's in the house, he won't hear 'im comin'. He says if he sleeps in the hay mow, the animals in the barn will let him know if anyone comes.'

Greta assumed the look of an affronted matron whose social graces were under fire. 'Why, I won't hear of it! I'll not be treating him like some saddle bum. Why even a saddle bum would be allowed to stay in the bunkhouse!'

'He won't stay otherwise,' Sam declared.

'Oh, that's nonsense!' Greta huffed. 'You'll stay in the house, won't you Tad?'

Tad paused between bites just long

enough to say, 'No, ma'am.'

Greta stared at him, mouth hanging open for several seconds. Frank intruded into her outrage. 'If he'd feel safer out there, I don't know as we'd oughta argue with 'im. Greta, you get some blankets an' such. I'll holler at Lame and have him get the boy bedded down in the mow.'

Greta clearly wanted to argue the point, but pushed away from the table and huffed out of the room instead. By the time she returned, Tad had finished his third plate of food and was standing by the door, peering out at the growing dusk, clearly worried.

Lamech Farmer came to the door in response to Frank's yell. 'Lame,' Frank told the ranch-hand, 'I'd like you to take the lad out and fix him up a bed in the hay mow. And make sure everyone knows that nobody says a word about his bein' on the place. Even if somebody comes a-lookin' for 'im, we ain't seen 'im, we don't know where he's at, and we ain't sure there even is anyone by that name in Wyoming Territory.'

Lame gave his boss a long questioning look, but received no explanation. He shrugged his shoulders. To Tad he said, 'Well, I'd tell you to come with me, kid, but since there ain't no kid there to talk to, I guess I'll just meander off to the barn all by myself and lay out this here bed for nobody up in that hay mow where there ain't gonna be anybody sleepin' in it.'

As he strode off following the cowboy, Tad turned and flashed Sam the first smile he had ever seen on the boy's face. He watched as the duo disappeared into the barn, then turned to find Dorrie standing close beside him.

'I've never seen anybody that size eat that much,' Dorrie said. 'Where in the world does he put it?'

Sam shrugged. 'I don't know, but he ate some jerky and dried biscuits o' mine, then Cap gave 'im some bacon and a lard sandwich before we headed over here.'

Dorrie looked at him as if struggling to believe what he said. 'You're serious?'

'Plumb serious.'

'He must have been half starved.'

'I 'spect. He's been too scared of whoever it is he thinks is gonna kill 'im to stop and eat.'

'Let's go for a walk,' she suggested.

His heart leaped at the thought of being alone with Dorrie, but he tried his best to appear nonchalant. 'Sure. Anyplace in particular?'

She shrugged. 'No. I just want some time with you. I haven't seen you since —'

'Yesterday,' he offered.

'Was it just yesterday?' she pretended surprise. 'I thought it was a lot longer than that.'

'Sure seems like a lot longer, all right,' he agreed.

As they stepped off of the porch, Dorrie slipped her hand into his. He laced his fingers between hers, and felt the magic of her touch tingle its way through his whole body. The minute they were into the trees along the creek, out of sight of the ranch yard, she turned and threw her arms around his neck. Their lips met in a long, lingering kiss Sam didn't want to ever end. It did, but was almost immediately followed by another. Dorrie lowered her head finally and lay it against his chest. He held her close, his face buried in her hair, one hand moving slowly up and down her back.

'Oh, Sam, you could have been killed last night.'

'That's all I could think about,' he murmured into her hair, 'that if they hung me, I'd never get to see you again.'

She pulled back from him just enough to look up into his eyes in the growing dusk. 'I love you, Sylvester Anthony Murray!'

He chuckled. 'Now why does that sound more like teasing than serious?'

'Why? Because I called you by your real name?'

'Yeah. Nobody calls me that without smilin'.'

'How about if I just kiss you instead?'

'That'd be even better.'

It was. 'Mmm,' he said, 'you can call me Sylvester all you want if you do that every time.'

'Well?' she suddenly demanded.

'Well what?'

'I said, 'I love you, Sylvester Murray.''

'See now? You said it again. That means I get another kiss, right?'

'No! That means you're supposed to say something now.'

There was barely enough light left for her to see his eyes were dancing. His voice, however, carried an air of bland ignorance. 'Oh? Well, OK. Let's see, what should I say? I know. 'Kiss me again.''

'Wrong thing! Try again.'

'Oh. Well, how about, 'It's sure a fine evening'?'

'Try again.'

'I sure do like the way your hair feels and smells.'

'Sam Murray! You know good and well what I mean! I want to hear you say it.'

'Oh, OK. 'It.' There. It's just a two-letter word. I don't see what was such a big deal about that.'

She stomped on his toe. 'Ouch!' he complained.

'Say it!'

'I said 'it'.'

She stomped on his toe again, then turned as if to flounce away.

He grabbed her by the shoulders and turned her around. He looked deeply into her eyes as his hand brushed downward across the side of her face, his fingers trailing along the line of her jaw. His voice was soft, husky, as he said, 'I love you, too, Dorene Marie Birdwell.'

'What did you say?'

'You didn't hear me?'

'Oh, I heard you perfectly well, I just wanted to hear it again.'

'I love you, I love you, I love you.'

He might have said it several more times, but her lips got in the way.

15

'I wanta know where my boy is.'

Mort Halverson stared at Gar Newberry. He made no pretense of friendliness. 'If ever a kid had reason to run away, I 'spect that boy does,' he declared. 'He ain't here, though, and I ain't seen 'im.'

Gar glared at the rancher a long moment. He had backed himself into a corner. If he demanded to search the house or any other part of the ranch, it would be tantamount to calling Mort a liar. If he did that, he would have to kill the rancher or be killed. In a country without lawyers and courts, all deals were made and sealed on the basis of a man's word. If a man's word wasn't any good, he had no way to do business. To call a man a liar, therefore, was more than just an insult to his integrity; it was a direct threat to his ability to function.

As a result, any man who was called a liar had to defend his honor instantly and violently. He either had to beat the one who accused him into retracting the comment and apologizing for it, or be beaten in the attempt. Just as likely, the one being called a liar would instantly go for his gun, and one or the other would die.

Newberry was smart enough to know that there were probably other eyes watching him at that very moment — he was not a popular figure in the area. Whatever hands were at the headquarters of the Circle T ranch would have noted his arrival. It was likely that even now one or more of the hands were watching him over the barrel of a rifle.

His voice taking on a more defensive tone, Newberry said, 'He's got no call to run off. I take good care of him.'

'From what I hear you treat him worse than a stray dog.'

'Now that just ain't true. I admit, I'm

a bit hard on 'im, from time to time. But that's 'cause I want 'im to grow up right an' be a man. Spare the rod and spoil the child.'

'There's a difference between spankin' a lad when he needs it and the kind of beating you're known to give that boy.'

'That's my business, how I discipline my own kid.'

'Up to a point, I'll allow that's true. But you'd just as well know most folks think you way overdo it. If the boy ever does show up here I'll give him a place to live for as long as he wants it, and I'll sure never tell you where he is.'

Newberry stared hard at the rancher for a long moment, then lifted his reins, turned his horse, and trotted out of the yard without another word. Mort watched him out of sight, then turned toward the barn and hollered, 'Ed!'

In minutes his foreman emerged from the blacksmith shop next to the barn. He leaned a rifle against the building and bowlegged his way across the yard. 'Yeah, boss?'

'Do you know anything about the Newberry kid?' Mort demanded.

Ed pursed his lips a long moment before answering. Then he said, 'Well, I do know Newberry's awful hard on the kid. Everybody in town knows that.'

'Do you know anything about him runnin' away?'

Ed hesitated again. 'Well, now, I can't say that I've seen 'im.'

'That's not what I asked.'

'So far as I know, he ain't nowhere on Circle T land.'

'Ed, you're fishin' awful hard for words to keep from answerin' my question.'

'Well, I don't guess I wanta answer it, to be right honest.'

'Why not?'

'Well, if'n I was to go blabbin' everything I know, it might cause that boy some serious problems, not to mention maybe other folks that I don't wanta be responsible for bringin' trouble on to.'

'Does it have to do with that new hand? The one that whipped Newberry for beatin' the kid?'

'Well, now, I ain't sayin' it does and I ain't sayin' it don't.'

'If he's gettin' himself in between Newberry and his kid, he's walkin' on some pretty dangerous ground.'

Ed thought about his answer carefully. 'Well, mind you, I still ain't sayin' I know anything, or that Sam's anyway involved, but if'n he was, I'd say he's likely able to take care of himself just fine.'

'He can take care of himself all right,' Mort agreed, 'but what about the Birdwell family? Knowin' how gossip gets around in this country, I'm guessin' the whole country knows he's sweet on the Birdwell girl.'

'There sure ain't no secret about that no more,' Ed agreed.

'Which means if he's involved, that's most likely where he'd take the kid, if he's hidin' 'im.'

'I couldn't say whether that might be the case or not.'

'I sent him with you, Cap, an' Lennie

to move them steers the other day. Are they in on this?'

'I couldn't say about that neither, boss.'

Mort's expression swayed back and forth between anger and hurt. Finally he said, 'Since when do you not trust me, Ed?'

Ed's expression reflected his own inner turmoil. 'It ain't that at all, Mort. I'd trust you with my life. You know that. If you tell me somethin', I know I can take it to the bank. But if I don't tell you somethin' you ain't supposed to know about, then you can straight out tell Newberry you don't know nothin' about it.'

Mort's face softened. 'You don't think I can handle Newberry?'

'Not without killin' 'im. You ain't as young as you used to be, Mort.'

'I can still handle myself.'

'You can still kill 'im, if you need to,' Ed agreed, 'but there ain't many that can stand up to Newberry in a stand-up fight.'

Mort looked inclined to argue the point, but changed his mind. 'He'll figure it out, quick enough. You do know that, don't you?'

'You reckon?'

'He ain't dumb. Murray's the one that stuck his nose in between him and his kid. Murray's the one that put the whoppin' on 'im like nobody else's ever managed to do. Murray's the most likely one for the kid to turn to if he's tryin' to run away from his ol' man.'

Ed bit his lip thoughtfully for a while, then said, 'Well then, there's somethin' else you maybe oughta know.'

Mort stared at him wordlessly, waiting for him to spill whatever else he had been hiding. 'It mighta been Newberry that tried to lay the Jew's murder onto Murray.'

'What? How?'

'When you sent Murray up to Clear Crick to camp out an' wait for me an' Cap an' Lennie, there was a posse showed up there accusin' him o' killin' Lowenstein.'

'What? They accused Murray of that? He wasn't even in town when that happened.'

'Yeah, I know that. But it was just like when that other posse lynched Eff. Newberry acted like he was plumb sure there'd be somethin' o' Lowenstein's in Murray's saddle-bag. Only there wasn't. They looked, but when there wasn't nothin' there, they went back to town, all mad at Gar for their wild goose chase.'

'So what makes you think that had something to do with Newberry tryin' to get even with Sam?'

'I figure Newberry mighta put somethin' in the saddle-bag afore he led the posse up there.'

'But there wasn't anything there, you said.'

'There wasn't when they looked. But there had been.'

Mort stared at his foreman in total confusion. 'Maybe you'd best stop playin' games and tell me what's goin' on.'

Ed took a deep breath. 'After the posse left, Newberry's kid come out've the timber and told Sam he'd taken that thing Lowenstein always wore around his neck out've Sam's saddle-bag. He said somebody besides his dad put it there, and that somebody else is the one that killed Lowenstein. But he wouldn't tell Sam who that somebody else is. I figure the boy's just coverin' for his old man. But he's betwixt a rock an' a hard place. Sam went to bat for him when the old man was beatin' on 'im, so he didn't want Sam gettin' hung for what his own dad did.'

Mort digested the glut of information, scowling, lips pursed. Finally he said, 'But the kid said Gar didn't do it.'

'Well, o' course he did. What kid's gonna squeal on his own pa?'

Mort visibly fought to find a better explanation, but couldn't think of one. He had to agree with everything his foreman had concluded.

'So it's pretty much boiled down to

bein' a feud goin' on between New-berry and Sam,' he observed. 'That means Newberry's gotta figure Sam's involved with the kid runnin' away, and probably hidin' 'im. Since the kid ain't here, he'll head for the Gadfly next.'

'That's what I'm afraid of,' Ed agreed.

'Send Sam up there to let 'em know. Make sure they're on the lookout for trouble. Tell 'im not to worry about gettin' back here till he knows every-thing's cleared up.'

'I won't be able to do that for another day or so.'

'Why not?'

'I sent 'im into town today with that sorrel stud. He's swellin' up some around his left front hock. He's too valuable for a stud to take any chances with 'im, so I had Sam take 'im into town for Moose to have a look at him.'

Mort frowned. 'Well, if anyone can take care of his problem, Moose can, but I ain't too keen on waitin' another day to get word up to the Birdwells.'

'I could maybe send Percy into town to pass the word to Sam.'

'Yeah, maybe you'd better,' Mort agreed. He took a deep breath. 'Then maybe you can send Cap and Lennie off somewhere to take a message to somebody else, instead o' takin care o' stock. We seem to be runnin' a messenger service here instead of a ranch anyway.'

There didn't seem to be any point in responding to his boss's grousing, so Ed just turned and headed across the yard to send Percy on his quest.

16

It was a slow trip to town. Sam had it all figured out when he left the Circle T. If he rode hard into town, he could leave the stud with Moose at the livery barn, then make a quick ride out to the G Bar F, have an hour or two to spend with Dorrie, then make it back to town in time to take the stud back home.

Things almost never work out the way men plan, however. Especially when the man planning is too much in love to think with his head instead of his heart.

The stud was limping too badly for the trip to be a hurried one. He was too valuable as a stud to make him put unnecessary pressure on the ailing leg. Struggling with his own impatience, he was forced to make the trip into town at a slow walk. It was well past noon when he finally rode down the main street of

Big Springs and reined in before the livery barn.

'Stud's lame,' Moose commented, as if he had been watching their approach.

'Yeah, he's got somethin' wrong with his left front leg,' Sam explained, knowing as he did that he was mouthing something the hostler had figured out on his own when they were still a hundred yards away.

Moose rubbed the sorrel's nose, speaking softly to him. He moved around to the side, stroking the horse, speaking soothingly to him. He rubbed around his ear, then scratched the side of his neck, moving his hand slowly down toward the swollen hock. He moved his hand softly across the swollen area. The horse moved the hoof away from him twice, but made no effort to kick or back away.

'It is not a snake bite. It is not a spider bite. I do not see any cuts. I think maybe it is cactus,' Moose said, speaking softly, the slow words blending in seamlessly with the soothing patter with which he kept the horse as calm as possible.

'Cactus?'

Harold explained, the pace of his words slow and carefully pronounced. 'I am just guessing, mind you, but I think so. I think maybe some sort of sticker got busted off. Then it started to fester and swell up. That made it swell over the top of the sticker, so it does not show.'

'So you'll have to dig it out?'

Harold nodded. 'I will need to do that. I will need for you to help me get him inside and tie up the back leg on the other side. That way he will not be able to kick me. After I get the sticker out, I will need to put a poultice on it.'

'Why don't we just tie up the sore one? Then it'll be up a ways where you can work on it easier anyway.'

Harold shook his head vigorously. 'No. I do not want to do that. If I tie up the sore leg, the rope would be right where it is the sorest. That would hurt him more than just digging out the sticker will hurt him.'

Sam fought a momentary urge to argue. He knew that if they had figured out the problem at the ranch, one of the hands would have thrown a loop over one of the stud's front legs and thrown him to the ground. Then another would have grabbed an ear and put his knee on the horse's neck, to prevent him from getting up. Others would have bound the horse's legs so he couldn't get up or kick. Then, with him flat on the ground, they would have poked and prodded until they found the offending sticker.

Fussing silently at the extra time it would take to do it the hostler's way, he led the stud and his own mount inside the livery barn. By the time he looped the reins of his own horse over the front rail of a stall, Harold had already looped the right hind leg, lifted it well off the ground, and tied it in a loop around the stud's neck. Sam made it to his side just in time to watch him expertly tie the rope in a bowline knot to keep it from tightening on the stud's neck if he fought it.

Slipping under the stud's neck, he squatted beside the left front leg. A knife appeared in his hand as if it had suddenly sprouted there from nowhere. He continued his crooning talk as the point of the knife penetrated the spot he had identified as the site of the sticker.

As if by magic, a spurt of yellow pus emerged from the side of the horse's hock. Reaching into the middle of it with a thumb and index finger, Harold tugged carefully for a moment, then held up a three-quarter-inch piece of cactus sticker.

'It almost squirted all the way out all by itself,' he said.

'How'd you know the exact spot to poke it, Moose?' Sam asked, a measure of awe showing in his voice.

Harold grinned. 'I think maybe I just have a way to see things like that,' he said. 'My wife says it is a gift. She says I have a way with animals, especially with horses.'

'Well, I sure can't argue with that.'

'I will need to put a poultice on his leg, though, so that it does not putrefy. It maybe would not need it, but I will feel better if you let me do that.'

'If you think that's what he needs, I sure ain't gonna argue with you. Do you want me to leave him for a day or two?'

'It would be a good idea, if you think Mr Halverson will not mind it costing him to board the horse for that long.'

'He'll make it right with you the next time he's in town,' Sam promised.

Sam walked out of the livery barn leading his own horse, fraught with indecision. He wanted in the worst way to ride straight to the G Bar F. At the same time, he had lost his excuse for not riding straight back to the Circle T. He sighed heavily and stepped into the saddle, turning his horse up the street. He stepped off in front of the café. He could at least eat a bite before he headed back. It had been a long time since breakfast.

He finished off the excellent meal, paid his ticket, and stepped back into the street. He looked for a long moment at the Lucky Drover. The bench in front of the saloon stood empty. Looking in through the open door, he could see no sign of activity. Still, the interior looked cool and inviting. Maybe he could have a beer before he headed back to the ranch.

His attention was abruptly attracted to a small dust cloud approaching from the direction of the Circle T.

'Somebody's in a hurry,' he muttered. 'Now what's up?'

He stood beside his horse, watching and waiting. 'Rides like Percy,' he observed moments later.

As the rider drew nearer, his observation was confirmed. He stood where he was until the Circle T hand slid his horse to a stop in the street next to him.

'You're ridin' that horse to a lather,' Sam remonstrated.

'You're s'posed to head for the

Gadfly in a hurry,' Percy blurted.

Sam was still accustomed to the hostler's overly slow, careful speech. It took him a couple seconds to digest the much-too-fast flurry of words from the cowboy. As the words soaked in, his heart plunged into his stomach. 'Why?'

'Newberry showed up lookin' for his kid,' Percy rattled hurriedly. 'He figures you're behind the kid runnin' off somewheres. Mort figures he'll head for the Gadfly next, seein' as how you're all sweet on that Birdwell girl.'

Sam had heard enough. An instant later he was in the saddle, spurring his horse to a dead run. 'He'd better slow down some or his horse won't make it all the way there,' Percy muttered.

He sat his horse watching Sam out of sight. Then he shrugged. Well, at least there was no reason for him to hurry back to the ranch. It'd be too late to do much by the time he got there anyway.

He dismounted, looped the reins of his horse around the hitch rail and walked into the Lucky Drover.

17

He had to slow his horse. At this pace, the animal would never make it to the Gadfly. His heart, hammering in his chest, refused to listen to what his mind well knew.

Mile after mile flew by beneath the great gelding's hooves. Sweat soaked first his flanks, then his chest, then his entire body was swathed in its salty coating.

His ears laid back tightly against his head. His nostrils flared. His head thrust forward, ever eager to force his body to greater effort for his master. His gait began to be visibly more labored. Foam flew from the corners of his mouth, around the bit.

An errant gust of wind whipped a bit of that foam so that it struck Sam in the face. He started as if he had been hit by something more substantial. His attention was finally arrested by his mount's labored stride.

Wrenched with conflicting needs, he reined the animal in, slowing him to a fast trot. The gelding tossed his head, insisting on his willingness to keep running if his master so desired. The noble animal would have done so until he ran himself to death.

Letting him do so would be more than cruel; it would be self-defeating. He had no chance at all to reach the Gadfly in time on foot. He probably would be too late in any case.

He had paid too little attention to his horse until he was badly winded. Then his attention was too much focused on the horse when he realized what his neglect was costing the creature. He leaned forward to pat the loyal beast on the neck. It took an instant for him to realize that his hat was knocked from his head as he did so.

An instant later, the sound of a rifle

shot slapped against his ears. Instinctively he jerked his rifle from its scabbard as he dived from the saddle.

A second bullet sizzled past his ear as he dived. The roar of the rifle that fired it was lost in the noise of his impact with the ground. He tucked his shoulder and rolled.

As his feet rolled back beneath him, he lunged sideways into another dive. As he did, he spotted a large soapweed. The dirt that had blown in around its base had, over the years, formed a mound nearly three feet high from which the spiny leaves of the plant reached skyward. Sam scrambled behind the welcome shelter of the dirt and roots.

Even as he did, another bullet kicked up dirt just behind his feet. He levered a shell into the chamber of his rifle and raised his head enough to peer between the narrow, jagged leaves of the yucca.

A hundred yards ahead of him a jumble of boulders formed the tip of a small hogback that jutted out from a ridge. He caught a fleeting glimpse of a hat moving away from him within that tangle of giant rocks.

As if of its own volition, his rifle jerked to his shoulder and barked. The hat sailed into the air. He knew, even as he squeezed the trigger, that he had allowed his aim to be drawn to the hat, instead of shooting just below it. Because his bullet would have knocked the hat the same direction his assailant was fleeing, he would probably even be able to pick it up as he ran.

Discretion demanded that Sam remain where he was, watch, and wait. He knew the one who had tried to ambush him might very well turn back into the rocks, gambling that Sam would think he was long gone. Then, when he left his cover, he would be an easy target.

At the same time he felt the slipping away of precious minutes. If Newberry had headed for the Gadfly instead of waiting for him to leave his cover, he would arrive there too far ahead of Sam for him to offer the Birdwells either warning or protection.

It came down to a decision in favor of his own safety or that of the Birdwells — especially Dorrie. That made the choice an easy one.

He gathered his feet beneath himself, careful to expose nothing to the gunman, in the event he was still there. He left the cover of the yucca in a dead run.

No shots rang out.

He reached his horse, still standing, head hanging, near exhaustion. He leaped into the saddle, slamming the rifle into its scabbard even as he hit the leather.

The horse responded as if he had been waiting all day for a little exercise. He leaped forward so quickly that Sam was nearly unhorsed. He grabbed the saddle-horn to catch his balance, then leaned forward, catching the animal's rhythm and moving with it.

He let the horse run for less than a hundred yards, then slowed him. By slowing down he knew he was making himself an irresistible target, if the gunman was waiting. He also knew his horse couldn't run much more. What's more, he had to keep going the direction the gunman knew he was going. He felt more helplessly vulnerable than he had ever felt in his life.

He leaned far forward, the saddlehorn digging into his stomach, his head beside the horse's neck, making himself as small a target as possible. He kept the horse at a brisk trot, his feet carrying his weight in the stirrups, his knees automatically absorbing the bounce of the animal's gait.

He rode that way for nearly half a mile, waiting every second for the impact of a bullet, or, he desperately hoped, maybe the sound of one narrowly missing him. There was neither.

He frowned in concentration. Was it Newberry who had shot at him? If so, why had he broken off the attack and fled? What might have inspired him to a different tactic, when he had Sam thoroughly pinned down, with an exhausted horse, and only whatever ammunition the magazine of the rifle held?

It hit him like a blow. Dorrie! With a sudden conviction that struck him like a sledgehammer he intuited that the man would attack him by going after Dorrie.

He resisted the urge to spur his flagging horse to a run again. Better to trot all the way than let the horse run himself to death a mile or two short of his goal.

It seemed half a lifetime passed. In fact, it was nearly an hour before he spotted the buildings of the G Bar F yard. Nothing stirred in the yard or the corrals. Smoke drifted lazily from the cookhouse chimney. Nothing else moved.

He left the road and stopped behind a large clump of bushes. From their cover he studied the yard carefully. Nothing seemed out of place. Two dogs lay dozing in the middle of the yard. A horse in one of the corrals whinnied a greeting, possibly catching the scent of his own horse. Nothing whatever seemed amiss.

He reined his horse back into the road and nudged him back to a trot. As he entered the yard, Lamech Farmer, one of Frank's hands, strode out of the barn. He took note of Sam's lathered horse and hurried toward him. 'Sam,' he called as he crossed the yard. 'You've pertnear run that horse to death. What's wrong?'

Before the echo of his words had bounced from the sides of the buildings, Greta Birdwell stepped out onto the house porch. 'Sam! What's wrong?' she demanded.

Just then Frank rounded the corner of the bunkhouse and sized up the situation. As Sam's feet struck the ground he hollered, 'What's wrong, Sam?'

The sound of the thrice-repeated question bounced around inside the hollow pain of Sam's terror. His eyes darted all around the yard. He peered at every window in the house, desperately seeking the face that should be peering back at him. The blank stares of empty windows mocked his efforts.

'Where's Dorrie?' he demanded.

'She went for a ride a while ago,' Frank responded. 'Why?'

Instead of answering, Sam asked, 'Has Newberry been here?'

Frank shot a look at his wife, who looked just as confused as he. He looked back at Sam. 'No. We ain't seen nothin' of him. Why?'

'He showed up at the Circle T, demanding to know where his kid was. We figured he was headin' over here when he left. Then someone tried to bushwhack me about five miles back.'

'What? Are you OK? Who was it?'

'I'm fine. He missed, but barely. Missed me half a dozen times, to be exact. He just didn't have a sittin' target after the first shot. I shot his hat off, but I don't think I hit him.'

'Was it Newberry?'

'Couldn't see, but that's my guess. Which way'd Dorrie go?'

Frank gestured with his arm. 'She was gonna ride up along the ridge and take a look at the cows an' calves in the hollow on the other side.'

'How long's she been gone?'

Frank thought about it for a moment, his face becoming visibly more concerned as he thought. 'Long enough she shoulda been home by now, come to think about it,' he worried.

Sam turned to Lamech. 'Lame, could you grab me a horse quick I can switch my saddle to?'

Instead of answering, Lamech whirled and ran for the barn. Frank started to follow him. Sam's voice brought him up short. 'Let me go alone, Frank. One man has a better chance of following a trail without being noticed until he wants to be.'

Frank stopped. He stood teetering on his toes, leaning first toward the barn then back toward Sam. Finally he nodded, though with obvious doubts. 'I'll give you a thirty-minute start, then I'll follow you, just in case you need backup. Leave me a trail I can follow. My eyes ain't as sharp as they used to be.'

As he talked, Sam was hurriedly removing the saddle from his spent horse. As he pulled the saddle-blanket and pad off the lathered animal, Lamech trotted up with a big bay mare. Without a word Sam flung the blanket, pad, and saddle onto the fresh horse. As he did, Lamech removed the bridle from the gelding and put it on the mare, putting the halter that had been on her onto the gelding instead.

'I'll rub 'im down good and grain 'im,' he said.

'As soon as you do, saddle Tom for me,' Frank ordered. 'I'm givin' Sam a thirty-minute start then followin' him.'

'We both will,' Lamech countered as he led Sam's horse toward the barn.

Sam didn't respond. He was already in the saddle, heading out of the yard. It didn't even occur to him to ask about Tad.

18

He had never been much of a tracker. As with nearly all men who lived in sparsely settled, wild areas, he could recognize most tracks when he saw them. He could tell whether tracks were fresh or days old. He could spot a trail through tall grass or brush. He could even pick out a trail on more difficult terrain, given time.

There were men that could follow a trail across hard or rocky ground unerringly from horseback, even at a swift trot. Some were good enough it was said of them that they could track a fly across a granite cliff. He just was not among that elite class of men.

He headed out the direction Frank had indicated that Dorrie had ridden. It had rained recently enough that the ground was relatively soft. The grass was tall. He could clearly see the path her travels had taken her for more than a mile and a half. Then she had ridden into an area of timber. The ground was covered with dried pine needles. There was little or no grass or underbrush. It was as if her trail simply disappeared.

Sam sat the G Bar F horse he had been lent with a sinking feeling in his gut. With no other course of action clear to him, he continued riding in the same general direction Dorrie had been heading. He came out of the other side of the patch of timber and stopped, studying the ground on all sides. He could see no sign of her horse's passing.

He rode parallel to that edge of the timber, watching the tall grass for indication of where she had exited the trees. Half an hour later he found it. He had been scant yards from it when he emerged from the timber, but he had turned the wrong direction in search of her trail. Precious minutes had been wasted.

Even so, he was not confident enough to follow her trail at more than a trot. Keeping his eyes well ahead, he could see enough broken and trampled grass to keep on the general line of her travel. More than that he could not expect of himself.

He was another half mile when his heart stopped. He felt as if he had been kicked in the gut. The grass was smashed and trampled in a wide circle. Clearly something had transpired there, but he was at a complete loss to understand it. His gut told him Dorrie had encountered someone, that there had been a tussle of some sort, but nothing beyond that.

Looking beyond the trampled area, he could see the line of two sets of tracks, close together, leading away. Whatever had happened, it was apparent that Dorrie had ridden away with somebody. Whether of her own volition or not he had no way to know.

Trying his best to swallow his panic, he nudged the horse to a swift trot, following the twin tracks. He followed them for another half a mile, when the grass gave way to a gravelly slope. The scant bunch grass and rocks gave no clue he could see. He looked around frantically, trying his best to feel some mental bond that would tell him where the woman he loved had gone, or been taken.

His efforts served only to recall her face, her dancing eyes, the tilt of her head, her lilting laugh. He felt again the press of her body against him as she had tipped her head back to return his kisses. He remembered every detail of the way her hair curled against her ears, and the curve of her neck below the ear. He could see and feel and hear every detail of her, but he could capture no sense of the direction she had gone.

In desperation he once again rode in the direction the tracks had been going when they disappeared on the hard ground. He came to the edge of the timber where it reached out over the lip of a broad canyon and sat the saddle in total frustration. Should he descend into the canyon to try to find some sign of her and whomever she was with? Should he follow the edge of the canyon, hoping to see where they had passed? Had he guessed the completely wrong direction, and been moving farther and farther away from them, instead of closer?

'He took her that way.'

Sam nearly jumped out of his skin. His forty-five leaped into his hand. He twisted so hard in the saddle, a sharp pain stabbed along his ribs. There was nobody there.

'Who's there?' he demanded.

An instant later a shadow separated from the trunk of a large northern pine tree. Tad Newberry stood watching him solemnly. 'He took her that way,' the boy repeated, pointing behind himself.

'Who did?' Sam demanded.

'That guy. He jerked her off her horse. Then he hit her. Then he made her get back on her horse, an' he tied her hands to the saddle-horn. Then he led her horse an' rode off that way.'

'Where's he takin' her?'

Tad shrugged wordlessly.

'Can you follow 'em?'

Tad nodded. 'I can track good.'

'Then show me. Do you want to ride?'

The boy shook his head. 'I kin walk.'

Without another word he whirled and started off. He didn't walk. He ran. It wasn't a full run, but he loped easily at nearly the same speed Sam's horse trotted. He neither looked back nor hesitated. As if led by some unseen tether, he ran about an eighth of a mile back the way Sam had come, following the edge of the canyon.

A deer trail angled downward from the canyon's rim, barely visible because of the brush that grew along either side of it. Tad never slowed as he began to follow its descent.

Sam couldn't keep up. He had to let his horse pick her way slowly and carefully. Frequently branches crossed the trail low enough he had to flatten himself onto the horse's neck to keep from being swept from her back. Twice the trail crossed talus slopes where it seemed to disappear completely. Each time, Tad stood at the other side of the rocky area, waiting for Sam to catch up. If he hadn't, Sam would have lost the trail again.

It took half an hour to descend onto the floor of the canyon. The whole of the lower half of it lay in shadow. It was hushed and peaceful, as if the world and all its woes were shut away somewhere beyond the canyon's rim. The turmoil in Sam's breast belied that appearance and clashed with it so painfully he wanted to shout, to yell, to shoot his gun in the air — anything to rob the canyon of the serene facade it tried so hard to transmit.

Following signs Sam could catch no glimpse of, Tad continued at his uncannily swift pace. 'No wonder he could get out to Spring Crick and back to town so fast,' Sam marveled. 'That kid's like a deer. I wonder if he ever gets tired.'

He didn't, insofar as Sam could

discern. He kept on, following the bottom of the canyon. Deciduous trees mingled with the coniferous. Both were interspersed with buck brush, plum thickets, chokecherry bushes, and sundry flora thriving on the greater moisture level the canyon provided. At times the growth was so thick that Tad had to stop and wait for the horse and rider that followed him to work their way through and around. After more than a mile it began to broaden out.

Twice in a couple hundred yards Sam had clearly seen the tracks of two horses. One set was almost on top of the other, indicating the second horse was being led by the rider on the other. It was only those two glimpses of tracks that assured him the boy was, in fact, following the trail.

Ten yards in front of him, Tad stopped abruptly. He ducked behind a tree and motioned Sam back.

Sam jerked the mare's reins and slid from the saddle. He dropped the reins, knowing the horse would stand as if tied to the ground. As silently as possible he crept up even with Tad.

Wordlessly, Tad pointed. Moving back and forth to find a line of vision between branches of trees and brush, Sam finally spotted what the boy had seen.

On a flat spot a little ways up from the bottom of the canyon, a log cabin stood against the far canyon wall. Apparently built there by a trapper at some point, it looked as if it hadn't been used for a long time. One end of the roof sagged as if some of its supports had broken. Brush had grown up around it, nearly hiding it. The front door sagged on one hinge.

A few yards beyond the shack, two horses stood tied to trees. Sam recognized Dorrie's favorite pinto instantly.

'Are they inside?' Sam whispered.

He received no answer. He looked beside him, where Tad had been standing. The boy was nowhere to be seen.

'Now where'd he go?' Sam asked silently.

He thought about it briefly. He well knew the traumas the boy had endured. Now he had brought Sam to where his own father held the woman Sam loved, as a captive. How could he stand to stick around and see how things played out?

Sam had no doubt he was going to have to kill the boy's father. What would that do to Tad? Or quite possibly Gar might kill him. How would Tad react to that? What was it doing to the lad to know he was betraying his father? He had, in effect, chosen the man who had befriended him over his own flesh and blood. Would he, at the end, yell a warning to his father?

Sam shoved all the questions aside, striving to stuff the turbulence of their doubts beneath the level of his conscious thoughts. He strained to hear something from the cabin, but could discern nothing.

He mapped out a route from where he stood to the cabin door, noting each thing that might make enough noise to betray his approach, plotting a path around it. When he had finished doing so, he could contain himself no longer.

With silent steps but purposeful stride, he walked out of the shelter of the trees and crossed the bottom of the canyon.

'It's about time you showed up.'

The words slapped against Sam from off to his left. He whirled to face the sound.

He saw the gun first. The five-and-a-half inch barrel of the forty-four caliber Remington six-shooter pointed directly at his chest. It neither quivered nor wavered. Its barrel looked as large as the mouth of a cannon.

Sam's eyes followed upward to the gunman's face. His eyes opened wide. He stared in disbelief. He had been absolutely certain he would face Gar Newberry when he caught up to the pair Tad had been trailing. But it wasn't Newberry.

Felix Walker grinned at him over the Remington forty-four. There was no trace of blurriness in the man's eyes. He stepped closer to Sam, moving with catlike grace. There was no slur in his voice. 'Well, lookee who's all surprised at the town drunk,' Felix taunted.

'You!'

Walker laughed. 'Surprise, huh?'

Sam opened his mouth several times to speak, but couldn't calm the tumbled confusion of his thoughts enough to enunciate a rational question. Finally he said, 'Why?'

Walker shrugged. 'Why not? As long as everyone figures I'm just the town drunk, nobody pays me any attention at all. Holdin' up stages an' such is a mighty fine livin', as long as I don't have a posse on my tail. All I gotta do is slip back into town, slouch down on that bench in front o' the Lucky Drover, slop a little whiskey on my clothes, and laugh to myself at all the idiots chasin' themselves around in circles.'

Sam finally found his voice. 'But, but, it had to be Newberry that, that — '

Walker laughed again. 'Pretty good, huh? Wrapped a web around that blowhard that he ain't never gonna get out of now.'

'It was you that put that necklace in that cowboy's saddle-bag.'

'Of course it was.'

'Why? What did you have against him?'

Walker shrugged. 'Nothin'. He was just handy. I just mentioned to Newberry that they'd likely find somethin' from the holdup in his saddle-bag.'

'So why didn't he tell everyone why he knew where to find it?'

Walker laughed without humor again. ''Cause the conceited windbag don't never listen to anyone enough to know who said what. If everyone thinks I'm dead drunk, passed out at one o' them tables, they don't ever think that maybe I'm the one that said it. It's just a voice outa the crowd.'

'So why that cowboy?'

'Like I said, he was just handy. I

knew where he was campin', and it was close enough to town I could slip that necklace in his saddle-bag and get back into town without anyone noticin'. Then when they figured out they'd hung the wrong man, they'd blame Newberry. They was supposed to get mad enough about it to hang him too, but nobody had guts enough.'

'You wanted Newberry to get hung?'

'Well, well. The brilliant stranger finally figured it out.'

'Why?'

Walker's face turned hard, his voice flat. 'You let someone kick you on the way by every time he gets a chance, just because he thinks you're too drunk to know who done it. Every time that loudmouth bully kicked me on his way by I swore he'd pay one day. Now that day's finally come, and he's gonna pay.'

Sam's brain was spinning. 'You put that phil — whatever it is thing in my saddle-bag, too.'

'Of course I did. I still don't know how you found it and got it out of there before the posse got there, but I just done the same thing I had with the cowboy. Newberry'd had enough to drink I bet he still thinks it was his own idea that they'd find something of the Jew's in your saddle-bag. But you had a perfect alibi, so either before or after they hung you, they'd figure out you couldn'ta done it. So then they'd blame Newberry for sure.'

Sam knew his only chance was to keep the man talking, even though it was clear he wasn't going to have any kind of chance at all. He remembered all too clearly that when the man had decided to kill the woman on the stage, he had shot her in cold blood without hesitation. He also knew from the things he had heard that Lowenstein had been stabbed in the back. Whenever Walker grew tired of bragging, he would kill Sam just as swiftly and just as coldly.

'So now what? Trying to get Newberry killed hasn't worked.'

Walker chuckled quietly. Something

in the sound of the laugh sent chills down Sam's back. 'Oh, it's workin' just exactly like it's supposed to.'

'What d'ya mean?'

'I mean I've got him sewed up tighter'n a spinster's corset this time. I convinced him you're the one that's hidin' his kid. Then I sorta mentioned that you'd likely take him over to your heart-throb's place to hide him. Then I beat him out there and grabbed onto that little lady and brought her here. Now I'm gonna have me some real fun with her. When the guys that are followin' your trail get here and find her, what's been done to her is gonna be nasty enough the whole country'll be ready to hang the guy that did it. Then they'll find this here rabbit's foot that Gar always carries in his pocket right there on the floor beside her body.'

He held out his left hand, revealing the good luck charm that Newberry always carried.

Walker's smile disappeared. His eyes went flat. His voice was brittle as he said, 'That's more speech makin' than I've done in years. Now it's time to get rid o' you and go have some fun with that pretty little thing in the cabin.'

Sam braced for the bullet he knew would slam into his chest. He made the determination to ignore the bullet and live long enough to return the cold-blooded killer's fire. He tensed to draw his own weapon.

But just as Walker said the word, 'cabin,' a fist-sized rock slammed into the side of his head. At almost the same instant his Remington forty-four roared. Instead of slamming into his chest, Sam heard the angry whine of the bullet past his ear.

Within that same second, Sam's own forty-five roared and jumped in his hand. Before he saw the hole appear in Walker's shirt front, he had fired two more times. The second round made another hole in Felix's chest less than an inch from the first. The third shot struck him a couple inches higher, as he was propelled backward by the force of the first two bullets.

Sam didn't even stand to watch his adversary fall to the ground. He slammed his gun into its holster and whirled, running as fast as he could to the cabin.

From the corner of his eye he saw Tad watching from the edge of the trees, a second rock gripped in his hand, just in case he needed it. Sam reached the cabin and lunged through the door, then stopped, his eyes struggling to adapt to the near darkness of the interior.

Dorrie lay on a bedroll that had been spread on a hastily cleared patch of the cabin floor. A neckerchief was bound around her face, covering her mouth. Her feet were tied together. Her hands were tied behind her back.

The knife he didn't remember drawing from its sheath in his hand, Sam dropped to his knees beside her. The knife sliced through the ropes and the neckerchief as if they were soft butter. Dorrie spat a wad of cloth out of her mouth, her eyes wide with conflicting emotion. Then she was in his arms, sobbing, shaking, clinging to him as he picked her up from the floor. He held her against himself, turning slowly around and around, his face buried in her hair.

Movement in the doorway suddenly arrested Sam's attention. He flung Dorrie away and whipped out his forty-five, facing the door. Tad disappeared instantly from where he had been standing.

Sam holstered his gun immediately. 'Tad! Don't sneak up behind me that way! I mighta shot you!'

Tad peeked around the edge of the doorway, assuring himself that he wasn't about to be shot. Then he sidled into the cabin. Dorrie came back into Sam's arms again. 'How'd you find me?' Dorrie asked when she had controlled her emotions enough to talk.

'Tad trailed you,' Sam explained. 'I swear, he's a tracker, that kid is. Then he pegged Walker with a rock when he was about to shoot me.'

'I told you it wasn't my dad,' Tad accused.

Sam was once more at a loss for words. Finally he said, 'Yeah, you did. I thought you were just stickin' up for your dad. I'm sorry.'

Tad nodded once, as if that was all he needed to hear. He disappeared from the doorway.

19

'It was you that took a potshot at me,' Sam accused.

Gar Newberry glared belligerently back at Sam. He glanced around at the circle of accusing faces, and his expression lost its belligerence. 'I had a right. I thought you had my kid,' he said finally.

Sam's own expression mellowed. 'I did take him where you couldn't find 'im.'

'You had no call to do that.'

'Somebody needed to. Nobody has a right to beat a kid like that.'

'That's my business. You got no call to butt into someone else's family.'

Frank Birdwell spoke up. 'A man does have a right to raise his family as he sees fit,' he agreed, 'but there comes a time when somebody does need to butt in, Gar.' He kept his voice soft, slow, even, conciliatory. 'When a man lets himself get about so mad, sometimes he don't realize how hard he's bein' on a kid. Somebody needs to step in when that happens.'

Frank Birdwell, Lamech Farmer, Dorrie Birdwell, Gar Newberry, and Sam all sat their horses in a semicircle. Tad Newberry hung back in the edge of the timber, watching, as if ready to become that disappearing shadow once again if necessary. Felix Walker's body was tied across his own saddle. When that much had been accomplished, the group seemed uncertain what to do next. That somebody had to take the body into town and report to the marshal was obvious. Beyond that, nobody seemed to know who should do what, or when, or how.

Lamech Farmer had proven to be nearly as good a tracker as Tad. He and Frank had arrived at the hidden cabin minutes after Sam and Dorrie had moved out into the sunshine in the center of the canyon. Gar Newberry rode in scarce minutes behind them, after following them all the way from the G Bar F.

In the long and increasingly awkward silence, Gar took off his hat. He glared at Sam again. 'You put a hole in my good hat.'

Sam resisted the urge to put a second one right beside it. Instead he removed his own hat. 'Well, I guess that sorta makes us even. You put a hole in mine first.'

Unexpectedly Dorrie giggled. The pent-up intense emotions of the day finally got the better of her. Struggling valiantly to control her giggles, she said, 'You two sound just like two little kids in the school yard. 'You messed up my hat!' 'Well you messed up my hat first.''

'Well, he did,' Sam retorted.

Watching Dorrie struggle to control the giggles she couldn't stop, Sam finally turned to Gar. 'I reckon we'd oughta stop tryin' to kill each other,' he offered.

Instead of answering, Gar watched

Dorrie for a long moment as well. His truculent look slowly softened. He looked as if Dorrie's giggles were about to become contagious. 'Yeah, I 'spect.'

He reined his horse around. Ignoring all the others, he said, 'Let's go home, Tad.'

As if released by some hidden spring, Tad sprinted from the trees. Bounding like a deer, he leaped into the air and landed on the skirt of the saddle behind his father. He leaned forward, wrapped his arms around his father and laid his face against the big man's back. Without a word, Gar kicked his horse into motion. In seconds he was hidden by the trees and brush.

'Why in the world would the kid be that anxious to go with someone that uses him as hard as that?' Frank pondered.

Dorrie's answer was emphatic. 'Because he loves him. That's his father.'

'You reckon the man'll be any easier on 'im, after all this?' Lamech wondered.

In the silence that followed the question, Sam looked deeply into Dorrie's eyes. 'How about we just promise each other we'll do better with our kids?' he suggested.

Dorrie left no doubt about her approval of that idea.

THE END

We do hope that you have enjoyed reading this large print book.

Did you know that all of our titles are available for purchase?

We publish a wide range of high quality large print books including:
Romances, Mysteries, Classics
General Fiction
Non Fiction and Westerns

Special interest titles available in large print are:
The Little Oxford Dictionary
Music Book, Song Book
Hymn Book, Service Book

Also available from us courtesy of Oxford University Press:
Young Readers' Dictionary
(large print edition)
Young Readers' Thesaurus
(large print edition)

For further information or a free brochure, please contact us at:
Ulverscroft Large Print Books Ltd.,
The Green, Bradgate Road, Anstey,
Leicester, LE7 7FU, England.
Tel: (00 44) **0116 236 4325**
Fax: (00 44) **0116 234 0205**

Other titles in the
Linford Western Library:

KILL SLAUGHTER

Henry Remington

When a California train is robbed of $30,000, and two Pinkerton detectives are killed, bounty hunter James Slaughter rides to investigate. But a cloud of fear hangs over the railroad town of Visalia, and even the judge is running scared. Beaten up, jailed and framed by the sheriff's deputies, Slaughter survives assassination attempts — but is hit by still more trouble as a vicious range war erupts on the prairie . . .